THE AMETHYST BOX

LECTOR HOUSE PUBLIC DOMAIN WORKS

THE AMETHYST BOX

ANNA KATHARINE GREEN

ISBN: 978-93-90145-03-4

Published: -

LECTOR HOUSE LLP
E-MAIL: lectorpublishing@gmail.com

THE AMETHYST BOX

BY

ANNA KATHARINE GREEN

Author of The Millionaire Baby, The House in the Mist,
The Filigree Ball, etc., etc.

CONTENTS

Page

THE AMETHYST BOX

THE HOUSE IN THE MIST

THE RUBY AND THE CALDRON

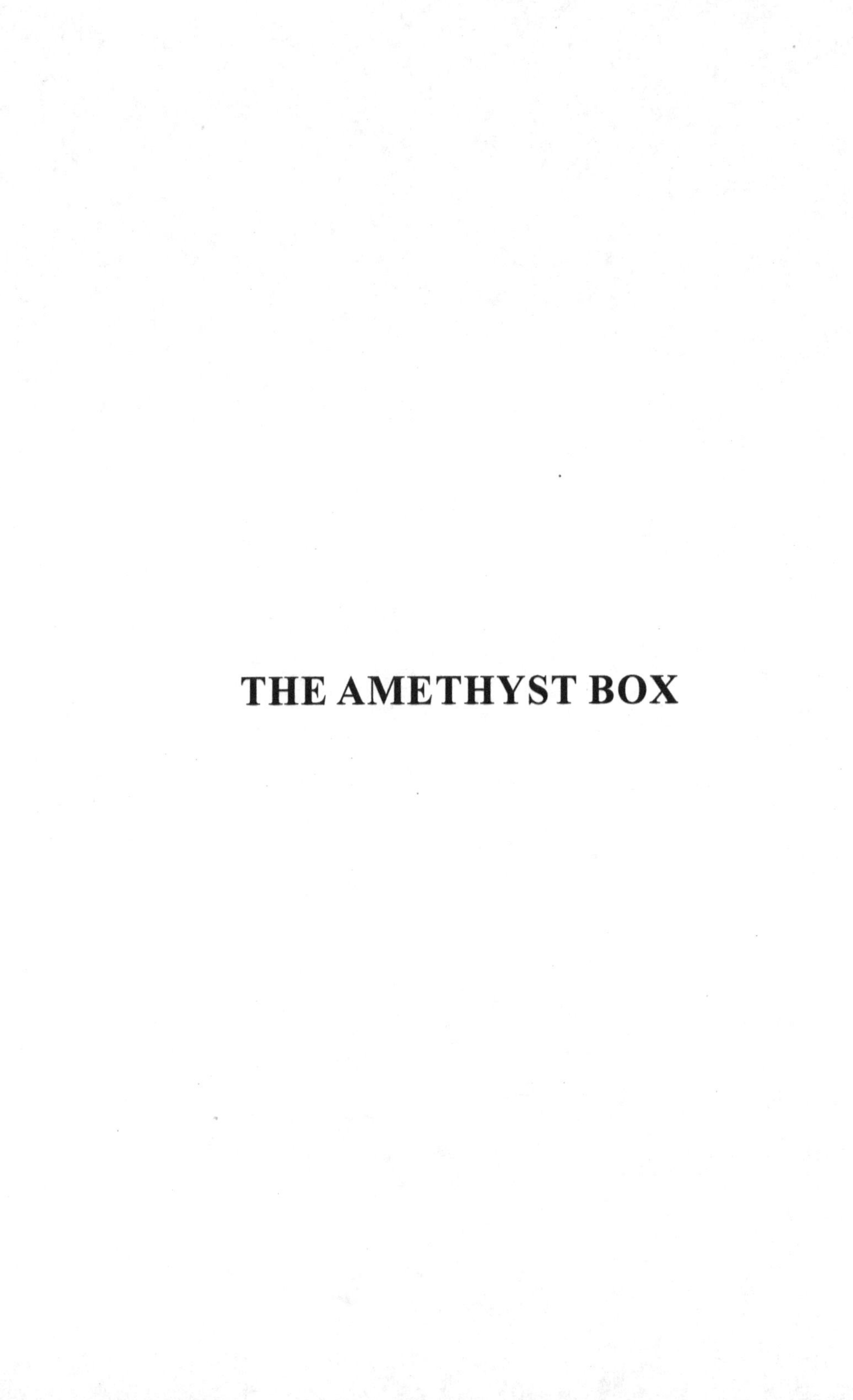

THE AMETHYST BOX

I

THE FLASK WHICH HELD BUT A DROP

It was the night before the wedding. Though Sinclair, and not myself, was the happy man, I had my own causes for excitement, and, finding the heat of the billiard-room insupportable, I sought the veranda for a solitary smoke in sight of the ocean and a full moon.

I was in a condition of rapturous, if unreasoning, delight. That afternoon a little hand had lingered in mine for just an instant longer than the circumstances of the moment strictly required, and small as the favor may seem to those who do not know Dorothy Camerden, to me, who realized fully both her delicacy and pride, it was a sign that my long, if secret, devotion was about to be rewarded and that at last I was free to cherish hopes whose alternative had once bid fair to wreck the happiness of my life.

I was reveling in the felicity of these anticipations and contrasting this hour of ardent hope with others of whose dissatisfaction and gloom I was yet mindful, when a sudden shadow fell across the broad band of light issuing from the library window, and Sinclair stepped out.

He had the appearance of being disturbed; very much disturbed, I thought, for a man on the point of marrying the woman for whom he professed to entertain the one profound passion of his life; but remembering his frequent causes of annoyance—causes quite apart from his bride and her personal attributes—I kept on placidly smoking till I felt his hand on my shoulder and turned to see that the moment was a serious one.

"I have something to say to you," he whispered. "Come where we shall run less risk of being disturbed."

"What's wrong?" I asked, facing him with curiosity, if not with alarm. "I never saw you look like this before. Has the old lady taken this last minute to—"

"Hush!" he prayed, emphasizing the word with a curt gesture not to be mistaken. "The little room over the west porch is empty just now. Follow me there."

With a sigh for the cigar I had so lately lighted I tossed it into the bushes and sauntered in after him. I thought I understood his trouble. The prospective bride was young—a mere slip of a girl, indeed—bright, beautiful and proud, yet with odd little restraints in her manner and language, due probably to her peculiar bringing up and the surprise, not yet overcome, of finding herself, after an isolated, if not despised, childhood, the idol of society and the recipient of general homage. The fault was not with her. But she had for guardian (alas! my dear girl had the same) an aunt who was a gorgon. This aunt must have been making herself disagreeable to the prospective bridegroom, and he, being quick to take offense, quicker than myself, it was said, had probably retorted in a way to make things unpleasant. As he was a guest in the house, he and all the other members of the bridal party—(Mrs. Armstrong having insisted upon opening her magnificent Newport villa for this wedding and its attendant festivities), the matter might well look black to him. Yet I did not feel disposed to take much interest in it, even though his case might be mine some day, with all its accompanying drawbacks.

But, once confronted with Sinclair in the well-lighted room above, I perceived that I had better drop all selfish regrets and give my full attention to what he had to say. For his eye, which had flashed with an unusual light at dinner, was clouded now, and his manner, when he strove to speak, betrayed a nervousness I had considered foreign to his nature ever since the day I had seen him rein in his horse so calmly on the extreme edge of a precipice where a fall would have meant certain death not only to himself, but also to the two riders who unwittingly were pressing closely behind him.

"Walter," he faltered, "something has happened, something dreadful, something unprecedented! You may think me a fool—God knows I would be glad to be proved so, but this thing has frightened me. I—" He paused and pulled himself together. "I will tell you about it, then you can judge for yourself. I am in no condition to do so. I wonder if you will be when you hear—"

"Don't beat about the bush. Speak up! What's the matter?"

He gave me an odd look full of gloom, a look I felt the force of, though I could not interpret it; then coming closer, though there was no one within hearing, possibly no one any nearer than the drawing-room below, he whispered in my ear:

"I have lost a little vial of the deadliest drug ever compounded; a Venetian curiosity which I was foolish enough to take out and show the ladies, because the little box which holds it is such an exquisite example of jewelers' work. There's death in its taste, almost in its smell; and it's out of my hands and—"

"Well, I'll tell you how to fix that up," I put in, with my usual frank decision. "Order the music stopped; call everybody into the drawing-room and explain the dangerous nature of this toy. After which, if anything happens, it will not be your fault, but that of the person who has so thoughtlessly appropriated it."

His eyes, which had been resting eagerly on mine, shifted aside in visible embarrassment.

"Impossible! It would only aggravate matters, or rather, would not relieve my fears at all. The person who took it knew its nature very well, and that person—"

"Oh, then you know who took it!" I broke in, in increasing astonishment. "I thought from your manner that—"

"No," he moodily corrected, "I do not know who took it. If I did, I should not be here. That is, I do not know the exact person. Only—" Here he again eyed me with his former singular intentness, and observing that I was nettled, made a fresh beginning. "When I came here, I brought with me a case of rarities chosen from my various collections. In looking over them preparatory to making a present to Gilbertine, I came across the little box I have just mentioned. It is made of a single amethyst and contains—or so I was assured when I bought it—a tiny flask of old but very deadly poison. How it came to be included with the other precious and beautiful articles I had picked out for her *cadeau*, I can not say; but there it was; and conceiving that the sight of it would please the ladies, I carried it down into the library and, in an evil hour, called three or four of those about me to inspect it. This was while you boys were in the billiard-room, so the ladies could give their entire attention to the little box which is certainly worth the most careful scrutiny.

"I was holding it out on the palm of my hand, where it burned with a purple light which made more than one feminine eye glitter, when somebody inquired to what use so small and yet so rich a receptacle could be put. The question was such a natural one I never thought of evading it, besides, I enjoy the fearsome delight which women take in the marvelous. Expecting no greater result than lifted eyebrows or flushed cheeks, I answered by pressing a little spring in the filigree-work surrounding the gem. Instantly, the tiniest of lids flew back, revealing a crystal flask of such minute proportions that the usual astonishment followed its disclosure.

"'You see!' I cried, 'it was made to hold *that*!' And moving my hand to and fro under the gas-jet, I caused to shine in their eyes the single drop of yellow liquid it still held. 'Poison!' I impressively announced. 'This trinket may have adorned the bosom of a Borgia or flashed from the arm of some great Venetian lady as she flourished her fan between her embittered heart and the object of her wrath or jealousy.'

"The first sentence had come naturally, but the last was spoken at random and almost unconsciously. For at the utterance of the word 'poison,' a quickly suppressed cry had escaped the lips of some one behind me, which, while faint enough to elude the attention of any ear less sensitive than my own, contained such an astonishing, if involuntary, note of self-betrayal that my mind grew numb with horror, and I stood staring at the fearful toy which had called up such a revelation of—what? That is what I am here to ask, first of myself, then of you. For the two women pressing behind me were—"

"Who?" I sharply demanded, partaking in some indefinable way of his excitement and alarm.

"Gilbertine Murray and Dorothy Camerden:"—his prospective bride and the woman I loved and whom he knew I loved, though I had kept my secret quite successfully from every one else!

The look we exchanged neither of us will ever forget.

"Describe the sound!" I presently said.

"I can not," he replied. "I can only give you my impression of it. You, like myself, fought in more than one skirmish in the Cuban War. Did you ever hear the cry made by a wounded man when the cup of cool water for which he has long agonized is brought suddenly before his eyes? Such a sound, with all that goes to make it eloquent, did I hear from one of the two girls who leaned over my shoulder. Can you understand this amazing, this unheard-of circumstance? Can you name the woman, can you name the grief capable of making either of these seemingly happy and innocent girls hail the sight of such a doubtful panacea with an unconscious ebullition of joy? You would clear my wedding-eve of a great dread if you could, for if this expression of concealed misery came from Gilbertine—"

"Do you mean," I cried in vehement protest, "that you really are in doubt as to which of these two women uttered the cry which so startled you? That you positively can not tell whether it was Gilbertine or—or—"

"I can not; as God lives, I can not. I was too dazed, too confounded by the unexpected circumstance, to turn at once, and when I did, it was to see both pairs of eyes shining, and both faces dimpling with real or affected gaiety. Indeed, if the matter had stopped there, I should have thought myself the victim of some monstrous delusion; but when a half-hour later I found this box missing from the cabinet where I had hastily thrust it at the peremptory summons of our hostess, I knew that I had not misunderstood the nature of the cry I had heard; that it was indeed one of secret longing, and that the hand had simply taken what the heart desired. If a death occurs in this house to-night—"

"Sinclair, you are mad!" I exclaimed with great violence. No lesser word would fit either the intensity of my feeling or the confused state of my mind. "Death *here*! where all are so happy! Remember your bride's ingenuous face! Remember the candid expression of Dorothy's eye—her smile—her noble ways! You exaggerate the situation. You neither understand aright the simple expression of surprise you heard, nor the feminine frolic which led these girls to carry off this romantic specimen of Italian deviltry."

"You are losing time," was his simple comment. "Every minute we allow to pass in inaction only brings the danger nearer."

"What! You imagine—"

"I imagine nothing. I simply know that one of these girls has in her possession the means of terminating life in an instant; that the girl so having it is not happy, and that if anything happens to-night it will be because we rested supine in the face of a very real and possible danger. Now, as Gilbertine has never given me reason to doubt either her affection for myself or her satisfaction in our approaching union, I have allowed myself—"

"To think that the object of your fears is Dorothy," I finished with a laugh I vainly strove to make sarcastic.

He did not answer, and I stood battling with a dread I could neither conceal nor avow. For preposterous as his idea was, reason told me that he had some grounds for his doubt.

Dorothy, unlike Gilbertine Murray, was not to be read at a glance, and her trouble—for she certainly had a trouble—was not one she chose to share with any one, even with me. I had flattered myself in days gone by that I understood it well enough, and that any lack of sincerity I might observe in her could be easily explained by the position of dependence she held toward an irascible aunt. But now that I forced myself to consider the matter carefully I could not but ask if the varying moods by which I had found myself secretly harrowed had not sprung from a very different cause—a cause for which my persistent love was more to blame than the temper of her relative. The aversion she had once shown to my attentions had yielded long ago to a shy, but seemingly sincere appreciation of them, and gleams of what I was fain to call real feeling had shown themselves now and then in her softened manner, culminating to-day in that soft pressure of my hand which had awakened my hopes and made me forget all the doubts and caprices of a disturbing courtship.

But, had I interpreted that strong, nervous pressure aright? Had it necessarily meant love? Might it not have sprung from a sudden desperate resolution to accept a devotion which offered her a way out of difficulties especially galling to one of her gentle but lofty spirit? Her expression when she caught my look of joy had little of the demure tenderness of a maiden blushing at her first involuntary avowal. There was shrinking in it, but it was the shrinking of a frightened woman, not of an abashed girl; and when I strove to follow her, the gesture with which she waved me back had that in it which would have alarmed a more exacting lover. Had I mistaken my darling's feelings? Was her heart still cold, her affection unwon? Or—thought insupportable!—had she secretly yielded to another what she had so long denied me and—

"Ah!" quoth Sinclair at this juncture, "I see that I have roused you at last." And unconsciously his tone grew lighter and his eye lost the strained look which had made it the eye of a stranger. "You begin to see that a question of the most serious import is before us, and that this question must be answered before we separate for the night."

"I do," said I.

His relief was evident.

"Then so much is gained. The next point is, how are we to settle our doubts? We can not approach either of these ladies with questions. A girl wretched enough to contemplate suicide would be especially careful to conceal both her misery and its cause. Neither can we order a search made for an object so small that it can be concealed about the person."

"Yet this jewel must be recovered. Listen, Sinclair. I will have a talk with Dorothy, you with Gilbertine. A kind talk, mind you! one that will soothe, not frighten. If a secret lurks in either breast our tenderness should find it out. Only, as you love me, promise to show me the same frankness I here promise to show you. Dear as Dorothy is to me, I swear to communicate to you the full result of my conversation with her, whatever the cost to myself or even to her."

"And I will be equally fair as regards Gilbertine. But, before we proceed to such extreme measures, let us make sure that there is no shorter road to the truth. Some one may have seen which of our two dear girls went back to the library after we all came out of it. That would narrow down our inquiry and save one of them, at least, from unnecessary disturbance."

It was a happy thought, and I told him so, but at the same time bade him look in the glass and see how impossible it would be for him to venture below without creating an alarm which might precipitate the dread event we both feared.

He replied by drawing me to his side before the mirror and pointing to my own face. It was as pale as his own.

Most disagreeably impressed by this self-betrayal, I colored deeply under Sinclair's eye and was but little, if any, relieved when I noticed that he colored under mine. For his feelings were no enigma to me. Naturally he was glad to discover that I shared his apprehensions, since it gave him leave to hope that the blow he so dreaded was not necessarily directed toward his own affections. Yet, being a generous fellow, he blushed to be detected in his egotism, while I—well, I own that at that moment I should have felt a very unmixed joy at being assured that the foundations of my own love were secure, and that the tiny flask Sinclair had missed had not been taken by the hand of the one to whom I looked for all my earthly happiness.

And my wedding-day was as yet a vague and distant hope, while his was set for the morrow.

"We must carry down stairs very different faces from these," he remarked, "or we shall be stopped before we reach the library."

I made an effort at composure, so did he; and both being determined men, we soon found ourselves in a condition to descend among our friends without attracting any closer attention than was naturally due him as prospective bridegroom and myself as best man.

II

BEATON'S DREAM

Mrs. Armstrong, our hostess, was fond of gaiety, and amusements were never lacking. As we stepped down into the great hall we heard music in the drawing-room and saw that a dance was in progress.

"That is good," observed Sinclair. "We shall run less risk of finding the library occupied."

"Shall I not look and see where the girls are? It would be a great relief to find them both among the dancers."

"Yes," said he, "but don't allow yourself to be inveigled into joining them. I could not stand the suspense."

I nodded and slipped toward the drawing-room. He remained in the bay-window overlooking the terrace.

A rush of young people greeted me as soon as I showed myself. But I was able to elude them and catch the one full glimpse I wanted of the great room beyond. It was a magnificent apartment, and so brilliantly lighted that every nook stood revealed. On a divan near the center was a lady conversing with two gentlemen. Her back was toward me, but I had no difficulty in recognizing Miss Murray. Some distance from her, but with her face also turned away, stood Dorothy. She was talking with an unmarried friend and appeared quite at ease and more than usually cheerful.

Relieved, yet sorry that I had not succeeded in catching a glimpse of their faces, I hastened back to Sinclair, who was watching me with furtive eyes from between the curtains of the window in which he had secreted himself. As I joined him a young man, who was to act as usher, sauntered from behind one of the great pillars forming a colonnade down the hall, and, crossing to where the music-room door stood invitingly open, disappeared behind it with the air of a man perfectly contented with his surroundings.

With a nervous grip Sinclair seized me by the arm.

"Was that Beaton?" he asked.

"Certainly; didn't you recognize him?"

He gave me a very strange look.

"Does the sight of him recall anything?"

"No."

"You were at the breakfast-table yesterday morning?"

"I was."

"Do you remember the dream he related for the delectation of such as would listen?"

Then it was my turn to go white.

"You don't mean—" I began.

"I thought at the time that it sounded more like a veritable adventure than a dream; now I am sure that it was such."

"Sinclair! You do not mean that the young girl he professed himself to have surprised one moonlit night standing on the verge of the cliff, with arms up-stretched and a distracted air, was a real person?"

"I do. We laughed at the time; he made it seem so tragic and preposterous. I do not feel like laughing now."

I gazed at Sinclair in horror. The music was throbbing in our ears, and the murmur of gay voices and swiftly moving feet suggested nothing but joy and hi-larity. Which was the dream? This scene of seeming mirth and happy promise, or the fancies he had conjured up to rob us both of peace?

"Beaton mentioned no names," I stubbornly protested. "He did not even call the vision he encountered a woman. It was a wraith, you remember, a dream-maid-en, a creature of his own imagination, born of some tragedy he had read."

"Beaton is a gentleman," was Sinclair's cold reply. "He did not wish to injure, but to warn the woman for whose benefit he told his tale."

"Warn?"

"He doubtless reasoned in this way. If he could make this young and proba-bly sensitive girl realize that she had been seen and her intentions recognized, she would beware of such attempts in the future. He is a kind-hearted fellow. Did you notice which end of the table he ignored when relating this dramatic episode?"

"No."

"If you had we might be better able to judge where his thoughts were. Proba-bly you can not even tell how the ladies took it?"

"No, I never thought of looking. Good God! Sinclair, don't let us harrow up ourselves unnecessarily! I saw them both a moment ago, and nothing in their man-ner showed that anything was amiss with either of them."

For answer he drew me toward the library.

This room was not frequented by the young people at night. There were two or three elderly people in the party, notably the husband and the brother of the lady of the house, and to their use the room was more or less given up after night-fall. Sinclair wished to show me the cabinet where the box had been.

There was a fire in the grate, for the evenings were now more or less chilly. When the door had closed behind us we found that this same fire made all the light there was in the room. Both gas-jets had been put out and the rich yet home-like room glowed with ruddy hues, interspersed with great shadows. A solitary scene, yet an enticing one.

Sinclair drew a deep breath. "Mr. Armstrong must have gone elsewhere to read the evening papers," he remarked.

I replied by casting a scrutinizing look into the corners. I dreaded finding a pair of lovers hid somewhere in the many nooks made by the jutting book-cases. But I saw no one. However, at the other end of the large room there stood a screen near one of the many lounges, and I was on the point of approaching this place of concealment when Sinclair drew me toward a tall cabinet upon whose glass doors the firelight was shimmering, and, pointing to a shelf far above our heads, cried:

"No woman could reach that unaided. Gilbertine is tall, but not tall enough for that. I purposely put it high."

I looked about for a stool. There was one just behind Sinclair. I drew his attention to it.

He flushed and gave it a kick, then shivered slightly and sat down in a near-by chair. I knew what he was thinking. Gilbertine was taller than Dorothy. This stool might have served Gilbertine if not Dorothy.

I felt a great sympathy for him. After all, his case was more serious than mine. The bishop was coming to marry him the next day.

"Sinclair," said I, "the stool means nothing. Dorothy has more inches than you think. With this under her feet, she could reach the shelf by standing tiptoe. Besides, there are the chairs."

"True, true!" and he started up; "there are the chairs! I forgot the chairs. I fear my wits have gone wool-gathering. We shall have to take others into our confidence." Here his voice fell to a whisper. "Somehow or by some means we must find out if either of them was seen to come into this room."

"Leave that to me," said I. "Remember that a word might raise suspicion, and that in a case like this—Halloo, what's that?"

A gentle snore had come from behind the screen.

"We are not alone," I whispered. "Some one is over there on the lounge."

Sinclair had already bounded across the room. I pressed hurriedly behind him, and together we rounded the screen and came upon the recumbent figure of Mr. Armstrong, asleep on the lounge, with his paper fallen from his hand.

"That accounts for the lights being turned out," grumbled Sinclair. "Dutton must have done it."

Dutton was the butler.

I stood contemplating the sleeping figure before me.

"He must have been lying here for some time," I muttered.

Sinclair started.

"Probably some little while before he slept," I pursued. "I have often heard that he dotes on the firelight."

"I have a notion to wake him," suggested Sinclair.

"It will not be necessary," said I, drawing back, as the heavy figure stirred, breathed heavily and finally sat up.

"I beg pardon," I now entreated, backing politely away. "We thought the room empty."

Mr. Armstrong, who, if slow to receive impressions, is far from lacking intelligence, eyed us with sleepy indifference for a moment, then rose ponderously to his feet and was, on the instant, the man of manner and unfailing courtesy we had ever found him.

"What can I do to oblige you?" he asked; his smooth, if hesitating tones, sounding strange to our excited ears.

I made haste to forestall Sinclair, who was racking his brains for words with which to propound the question he dared not put too boldly.

"Pardon me, Mr. Armstrong, we were looking about for a small pin dropped by Miss Camerden." (How hard it was for me to use her name in this connection only my own heart knew.) "She was in here just now, was she not?"

The courteous gentleman bowed, hawed, and smiled a very polite but unmeaning smile. Evidently he had not the remotest notion whether she had been in or not.

"I am sorry, but I am afraid I lost myself for a moment on that lounge," he admitted. "The firelight always makes me sleepy. But if I can help you," he cried, starting forward, but almost immediately pausing again and giving us rather a curious look. "Some one was in the room. I remember it now. It was just before the warmth and glow of the fire became too much for me. I can not say that it was Miss Camerden, however. I thought it was some one of quicker movement. She made quite a rattle with the chairs."

I purposely did not look back at Sinclair.

"Miss Murray?" I suggested.

Mr. Armstrong made one of his low, old-fashioned bows. This, I doubt not, was out of deference to the bride-to-be.

"Does Miss Murray wear white to-night?"

"Yes," muttered Sinclair, coming hastily forward.

"Then it may have been she, for as I lay there deciding whether or not to yield to the agreeable somnolence I felt creeping over me, I caught a glimpse of her skirt as she passed out of the room. And that skirt was white—white silk, I suppose you call it. It looked very pretty in the firelight."

Sinclair, turning on his heel, stalked in a dazed way toward the door. To cover this show of abruptness which was quite unusual on his part, I made the effort of my life, and, remarking lightly, "She must have been here looking for the pin her friend has lost," I launched forth into an impromptu dissertation on one of the subjects I knew to be dear to the heart of the bookworm before me, and kept it up, too, till I saw by his brightening eye and suddenly freed manner that he had forgotten the insignificant episode of a minute ago, never in all probability to recall it again. Then I made another effort and released myself with something like deftness from the long-drawn-out argument I saw impending, and, making for the door in my turn, glanced about for Sinclair. So far as I was concerned the question as to who had taken the box from the library was settled.

It was now half-past eight. I made my way from room to room and from group to group, looking for Sinclair. At last I returned to my old post near the library door, and was instantly rewarded by the sight of his figure approaching from a small side passage in company with the butler, Dutton. His face, as he stepped into the full light of the open hall, showed discomposure, but not the extreme distress I had anticipated. Somehow, at sight of it, I found myself seeking the shadow just as he had done a short time before, and it was in one of the recesses made by a row of bay trees that we came face to face.

He gave me one look, then his eyes dropped.

"Miss Camerden has lost a pin from her hair," he impressively explained to me. Then turning to Dutton he nonchalantly remarked. "It must be somewhere in this hall; perhaps you will be good enough to look for it."

"Certainly," replied the man. "I thought she had lost something when I saw her come out of the library a little while ago holding her hand to her hair."

My heart gave a leap, then sank cold and almost pulseless in my breast. In the hum to which all sounds had sunk, I heard Sinclair's voice rise again in the question with which my own mind was full.

"When was that? After Mr. Armstrong went into the room, or before?"

"Oh, after he fell asleep. I had just come from putting out the gas when I saw Miss Camerden slip in and almost immediately come out again. I will search for the pin very carefully, sir."

So Mr. Armstrong had made a mistake! It was Dorothy and not Gilbertine whom he had seen leaving the room. I braced myself up and met Sinclair's eye.

"Dorothy's dress is gray to-night; but Mr. Armstrong's eye may not be very good for colors."

"It is possible that both were in the room," was Sinclair's reply. But I could see that he advanced this theory solely out of consideration for me; that he did not really believe it. "At all events," he went on, "we can not prove anything this way; we must revert to our original idea. I wonder if Gilbertine will give me the chance to speak to her."

"You will have an easier task than I," was my half-sullen retort. "If Dorothy perceives that I wish to approach her she has but to lift her eyes to any of the half-dozen fellows here, and the thing becomes impossible."

"There is to be a rehearsal of the ceremony at half-past ten. I might get a word in then; only, this matter must be settled first. I could never go through the farce of standing up before you all at Gilbertine's side, with such a doubt as this in my mind."

"You will see her before then. Insist on a moment's talk. If she refuses—"

"Hush!" he here put in. "We part now to meet in this same place again at ten. Do I look fit to enter among the dancers? I see a whole group of them coming for me."

"You will in another moment. Approaching matrimony has made you sober, that's all."

It was some time before I had the opportunity, even if I had the courage, to look Dorothy in the face. When the moment came she was flushed with dancing and looked beautiful. Ordinarily she was a little pale, but not even Gilbertine, with her sumptuous coloring, showed a warmer cheek than she, as, resting from the waltz, she leaned against the rose-tinted wall and let her eyes for the first time rise slowly to where I stood talking mechanically to my partner.

Gentle eyes they were, made for appeal, and eloquent with a subdued heart language. But they were held in check by an infinite discretion. Never have I caught them quite off their guard, and to-night they were wholly unreadable. Yet she was trembling with something more than the fervor of the dance, and the little hand which had touched mine in lingering pressure a few hours before was not quiet for a moment. I could not see it fluttering in and out of the folds of her smoke-colored dress without a sickening wonder if the little purple box which was the cause of my horror lay somewhere concealed amid the airy puffs and ruffles that rose and fell so rapidly over her heaving breast. Could her eye rest on mine, even in this cold and perfunctory manner, if the drop which could separate us for ever lay concealed over her heart? She knew that I loved her. From the first hour we met in her aunt's forbidding parlor in Thirty-sixth Street, she had recognized my passion, however perfectly I had succeeded in concealing it from others. Inexperienced as she was in those days, she had noted as quickly as any society belle the effect produced upon me by her chill prettiness and her air of meek reserve under which one felt the heart-break; and though she would never openly acknowledge my homage and frowned down every attempt on my part at lover-like speech or attention, I was as sure that she rated my feelings at their real value, as that she was the dearest, yet most incomprehensible, mortal my narrow world contained. When, therefore, I encountered her eyes at the end of the dance I said to myself:

"She may not love me, but she knows that I love her, and, being a woman of sympathetic instincts, would never meet my eyes with so calm a look if she were meditating an act which must infallibly plunge me into misery." Yet I was not satisfied to go away without a word. So, taking the bull by the horns, I excused myself to my partner, and crossed to Dorothy's side.

"Will you dance the next waltz with me?" I asked.

Her eyes fell from mine directly and she drew back in a way that suggested flight.

"I shall dance no more to-night," said she, her hand rising in its nervous fashion to her hair.

I made no appeal. I just watched that hand, whereupon she flushed vividly and seemed more than ever anxious to escape. At which I spoke again.

"Give me a chance, Dorothy. If you will not dance come out on the veranda and look at the ocean. It is glorious to-night. I will not keep you long. The lights here trouble my eyes; besides, I am most anxious to ask you—"

"No, no," she vehemently objected, very much as if frightened. "I can not leave the drawing-room—do not ask me—seek some other partner—do, to-night."

"You wish it?"

"Very much."

She was panting, eager. I felt my heart sink and dreaded lest I should betray my feelings.

"You do not honor me then with your regard," I retorted, bowing ceremoniously as I became assured that we were attracting more attention than I considered desirable.

She was silent. Her hand went again to her hair.

I changed my tone. Quietly, but with an emphasis which moved her in spite of herself, I whispered: "If I leave you now will you tell me to-morrow why you are so peremptory with me to-night?"

With an eagerness which was anything but encouraging, she answered with suddenly recovered gaiety:

"Yes, yes, after all this excitement is over." And, slipping her hand into that of a friend who was passing, she was soon in the whirl again and dancing—she who had just assured me that she did not mean to dance again that night.

III

A SCREAM IN THE NIGHT

I turned and, hardly conscious of my actions, stumbled from the room. A bevy of young people at once surrounded me. What I said to them I hardly know. I only remember that it was several minutes before I found myself again alone and making for the little room into which Beaton had vanished a half-hour before. It was the one given up to card-playing. Did I expect to find him seated at one of the tables? Possibly; at all events I approached the doorway and was about to enter when a heavy step shook the threshold before me and I found myself confronted by the advancing figure of an elderly lady whose portrait it is now time for me to draw. It is no pleasurable task, but one I can not escape.

Imagine, then, a broad, weighty woman of not much height, with a face whose features were usually forgotten in the impression made by her great cheeks and falling jowls. If the small eyes rested on you, you found them sinister and strange, but if they were turned elsewhere, you asked in what lay the power of the face, and sought in vain amid its long wrinkles and indeterminate lines for the secret of that spiritual and bodily repulsion which the least look into this impassive countenance was calculated to produce. She was a woman of immense means, and an oppressive consciousness of this spoke in every movement of her heavy frame, which always seemed to take up three times as much space as rightfully belonged to any human creature. Add to this that she was seldom seen without a display of diamonds which made her broad bust look like the bejeweled breast of some Eastern idol, and some idea may be formed of this redoubtable woman whom I have hitherto confined myself to speaking of as *the gorgon*.

The stare she gave me had something venomous and threatening in it. Evidently for the moment I was out of her books, and while I did not understand in what way I had displeased her, for we always had met amicably before, I seized upon this sign of displeasure on her part as explanatory, perhaps, of the curtness and show of contradictory feelings on the part of her dependent niece. Yet why should the old woman frown on me? I had been told more than once that she regarded me with great favor. Had I unwittingly done something to displease her, or had the game of cards she had just left gone against her, ruffling her temper and making it imperative for her to choose some object on which to vent her spite? I entered the room to see. Two men and one woman stood in rather an embarrassed silence about a table on which lay some cards, which had every appearance of having been thrown down by an impatient hand. One of the men was Will Beaton, and it was he who now remarked:

"She has just found out that the young people are enjoying themselves. I wonder upon which of her two unfortunate nieces she will expend her ill-temper tonight?"

"Oh, there's no question about that," remarked the lady who stood near him. "Ever since she has had a reasonable prospect of working Gilbertine off her hands, she has devoted herself quite exclusively to her remaining burden. I hear," she impulsively continued, craning her neck to be sure that the object of her remarks was quite out of earshot, "that the south hall was blue to-day with the talk she gave Dorothy Camerden. No one knows what about, for the girl evidently tries to please her. But some women have more than their own proper share of bile; they must expend it on some one." And she in turn threw down her cards, which up till now she had held in her hand.

I gave Beaton a look and stepped out on the veranda. In a minute he followed me, and in the corner facing the ocean, where the vines cluster the thickest, we held our conversation.

I began it, with a directness born of my desperation.

"Beaton," said I, "we have not known each other long, but I recognize a man when I see him, and I am disposed to be frank with you. I am in trouble. My affections are engaged, deeply engaged, in a quarter where I find some mystery. You have helped make it." (Here a gesture escaped him.) "I allude to the story you related the other morning of the young girl you had seen hanging over the verge of the cliff, with every appearance of intending to throw herself over."

"It was as a dream I related that," he gravely remarked.

"That I am aware of. But it was no dream to me, Beaton. I fear I know that young girl; I also fear that I know what drove her into contemplating so rash an act. The conversation just held in the card-room should enlighten you. Beaton, am I wrong?"

The feeling I could not suppress trembled in my tones. He may have been sensitive to it or he may have been simply good-natured. Whatever the cause, this is what he said in reply:

"It was a dream. Remember that I insist upon its being a dream. But some of its details are very clear in my mind. When I stumbled upon this dream-maiden in the moonlight her face was turned from me toward the ocean, and I did not see her features then or afterwards. Startled by some sound I made, she crouched, drew back and fled to cover. That cover, I have good reason to believe, was this very house."

I reached out my hand and touched him on the arm.

"This dream-maiden was a woman?" I inquired. "One of the women now in this house."

He replied reluctantly.

"She was a young woman and she wore a long cloak. My dream ends there. I can not even say whether she was fair or dark."

I recognized that he had reached the limit of his explanations, and, wringing his hand, I started for the nearest window, which proved to be that of the music-room. I was about to enter when I saw two women crossing to the opposite doorway, and paused with a full heart to note them, for one was Mrs. Lansing and the other Dorothy. The aunt had evidently come for the niece and they were leaving the room together. Not amicably, however. Harsh words had passed, or I am no judge of the human countenance. Dorothy especially bore herself like one who finds difficulty in restraining herself from some unhappy outburst, and as she disappeared from my sight in the wake of her formidable companion my attention was again called to her hands, which she held clenched at her sides.

I was stepping into the room when my impulse was again checked. Another person was sitting there, a person I had been most anxious to see ever since my last interview with Sinclair. It was Gilbertine Murray, sitting alone in an attitude of deep, and possibly not altogether happy thought.

I paused to study the sweet face. Truly she was a beautiful woman. I had never before realized how beautiful. Her rich coloring, her noble traits and the spirited air, which gave her such marked distinction, bespoke at once an ardent nature and a pure soul.

I did not wonder that Sinclair had succumbed to charms so pronounced and uncommon, and as I gazed longer and noted the tremulous droop of her ripe lips and the faraway look of eyes which had created a great stir in the social world when they first flashed upon it. I felt that if Sinclair could see her now he would never doubt her again, despite the fact that the attitude into which she had fallen was one of great fatigue, if not despondency.

She held a fan in her hand, and as I stood looking at her she dropped it. As she stooped to pick it up, her eyes met mine, and a startling change passed over her. Springing up, she held out her hands in wordless appeal—then let them drop again as if conscious that I would not be likely to understand either herself or her mood. She was very beautiful.

Entering the room, I approached her. Had Sinclair managed to have his little conversation with her? Something must have happened, for never had I seen her in such a state of suppressed excitement, and I had seen her many times, both here and in her aunt's house when I was visiting Dorothy. Her eyes were shining, not with a brilliant, but a soft light, and the smile with which she met my advance had something in it strangely tremulous and expectant.

"I am glad to have a moment in which to speak to you alone," I said. "As Sinclair's oldest and closest friend, I wish to tell you how truly you can rely both on his affection and esteem. He has an infinitely good heart."

She did not answer as brightly and as quickly as I expected. Something seemed to choke her, something which she finally mastered, though only by an effort which left her pale, but self-contained and even more lovely, if that is possible, than before.

"Thank you," she then said, "my prospects are very happy. No one but myself knows how happy." And she smiled again, but with an expression which recalled to my mind Sinclair's fears.

I bowed; some one was calling her name; evidently our interview was to be short.

"I am obliged," she murmured. Then quickly, "I have not seen the moon to-night. Is it beautiful? Can you see it from this veranda?"

But before I could answer, she was surrounded and dragged off by a knot of young people, and I was left free to keep my engagement with Sinclair.

I did not find him at his post nor could any one tell me where he had vanished.

It was plain that his conduct was looked upon as strange, and I felt some anxiety lest it should appear more so before the evening was over. I found him at last in his room sitting with his head buried in his arms. He started up as I entered.

"Well?" he asked sharply.

"I have learned nothing decisive."

"Nor I."

"I exchanged some words with both ladies and I tackled Beaton; but the matter remains just about where it was. It may have been Dorothy who took the box and it may have been Gilbertine. But there seems to be greater reason for suspecting Dorothy. She lives a hell of a life with that aunt."

"And Gilbertine is on the point of escaping that bondage. I know; I have thought of that. Walter, you are a generous fellow;" and for a moment Sinclair looked relieved. Before I could speak, however, he was sunk again in his old despondency. "But the doubt," he cried, "the doubt! How can I go through this rehearsal with such a doubt in my mind? I can not and will not. Go tell them I am ill and can not come down again to-night. God knows you will tell no untruth."

I saw that he was quite beside himself, but ventured upon one remonstrance.

"It will be unwise to rouse comment," I said. "If that box was taken for the death it holds, the one restraint most likely to act upon the young girl who retains it will be the conventionalities of her position and the requirements of the hour. Any break in the settled order of things—anything which would give her a moment by herself—might precipitate the dreadful event we fear. Remember, one turn of the hand and all is lost. A drop is quickly swallowed."

"Frightful!" he murmured, the perspiration oozing from his forehead. "What a wedding-eve! And they are laughing down there; listen to them. I even imagine I hear Gilbertine's voice. Is there unconsciousness in it or just the hilarity of a distracted mind bent on self-destruction? I can not tell; the sound conveys no meaning to me."

"She has a sweet, true face," I said, "and she wears a very beautiful smile to-night."

He sprang to his feet.

"Yes, yes; a smile that maddens me; a smile that tells me nothing, nothing! Walter, Walter, don't you see that, even if that cursed box remains unopened and nothing ever comes of its theft, the seeds of distrust are sown thick in my breast, and I must always ask: 'Was there a moment when my young bride shrank from me enough to dream of death?' That is why I can not go through the mockery of this rehearsal."

"Can you go through the ceremony of marriage?"

"I must—if nothing happens to-night."

"And then?"

I spoke involuntarily. I was thinking not of him, but of myself. But he evidently found in my words an echo of his own thought.

"Yes, it is the *then*," he murmured. "Well may a man quail before that *then*."

He did go down stairs, however, and later on, went through the rehearsal very much as I had expected him to do, quietly and without any outward show of emotion.

As soon as possible after this the company separated, Sinclair making me an imperceptible gesture as he went up stairs. I knew what it meant, and was in his room as soon as the fellows who accompanied him had left him alone.

"The danger is from now on," he cried, as soon as I had closed the door behind me. "I shall not undress to-night."

"Nor I."

"Happily we both have rooms by ourselves in this great house. I shall put out my light and then open my door as far as need be. Not a move in the house will escape me."

"I will do the same."

"Gilbertine—God be thanked—is not alone in her room. Little Miss Lane shares it with her."

"And Dorothy?"

"Oh, she is under the strictest bondage night and day. She sleeps in a little room off her aunt's. Do you know her door?"

I shook my head.

"I will pass down the hall and stop an instant before the two doors we are most interested in. When I pass Gilbertine's I will throw out my right hand."

I stood on the threshold of his room and watched him. When the two doors were well fixed in my mind, I went to my own room and prepared for my self-imposed watch. When quite ready, I put out my light. It was then eleven o'clock.

The house was very quiet. There had been the usual bustle attending the separation of a party of laughing, chattering girls for the night, but this had not lasted long, for the great doings of the morrow called for bright eyes and fresh cheeks, and these can only be gained by sleep. In this stillness twelve o'clock struck and the first hour of my anxious vigil was at an end. I thought of Sinclair. He had given no token of the watch he was keeping, but I knew he was sitting with his ear to the door, listening for the alarm which must come soon if it came at all.

But would it come at all? Were we not wasting strength and a great deal of emotion on a dread which had no foundation in fact? What were we two sensible and, as a rule, practical men thinking of, that we should ascribe to either of these dainty belles of a conventional and shallow society the wish to commit a deed calling for the vigor and daring of some wilful child of nature? It was not to be thought of in this sober, reasoning hour. We had given ourselves over to a ghastly nightmare and would yet awake.

Why was I on my feet? Had I heard anything?

Yes, a stir, a very faint stir somewhere down the hall—the slow, cautious opening of a door, then a footfall—or had I imagined the latter? I could hear nothing now.

Pushing open my own door, I looked cautiously out. Only the pale face of Sinclair confronted me. He was peering from the corner of an adjacent passageway, the moonlight at his back. Advancing, we met in silence. For the moment we seemed to be the only persons awake in the vast house.

"I thought I heard a step," was my cautious whisper after a moment of intense listening.

"Where?"

I pointed toward that portion of the house where the ladies' rooms were situated.

"That is not what I heard," was his murmured protest, "what I heard was a creak in the small stairway running down at the end of the hall where my room is."

"One of the servants," I ventured, and for a moment we stood irresolute. Then we both turned rigid as some sound arose in one of the far-off rooms, only to quickly relax again as that sound resolved itself into a murmur of muffled voices. Where there was talking there could be no danger of the special event we feared. Our relief was so great we both smiled. Next instant his face and, I have no doubt, my own, turned the color of clay and Sinclair went reeling back against the wall.

A scream had risen in this sleeping house—a piercing and insistent scream such as raises the hair and curdles the blood.

IV

WHAT SINCLAIR HAD TO SHOW ME

This scream seemed to come from the room where we had just heard voices. With a common impulse, Sinclair and I both started down the hall, only to find ourselves met by a dozen wild interrogations from behind as many quickly opened doors. Was it fire? Had burglars got in? What was the matter? Who had uttered that dreadful shriek? Alas! that was the question which we of all men were most anxious to hear answered. Who? Gilbertine or Dorothy?

Gilbertine's door was reached first. In it stood a short, slight figure, wrapped in a hastily-donned shawl. The white face looked into ours as we stopped, and we recognized little Miss Lane.

"What has happened?" she gasped. "It must have been an awful cry to waken everybody so!"

We never thought of answering her.

"Where is Gilbertine?" demanded Sinclair, thrusting his hand out as if to put her aside.

She drew herself up with sudden dignity.

"In bed," she replied. "It was she who told me that somebody had shrieked. I didn't wake."

Sinclair uttered a sigh of the greatest relief that ever burst from a man's overcharged breast.

"Tell her we will find out what it means," he replied kindly, drawing me rapidly away.

By this time Mr. and Mrs. Armstrong were aroused, and I could hear the slow and hesitating tones of the former in the passage behind us.

"Let us hasten," whispered Sinclair. "Our eyes must be the first to see what lies behind that partly-opened door."

I shivered. The door he had designated was Dorothy's.

Sinclair reached it first and pushed it open. Pressing up behind him, I cast a fearful look over his shoulder. Only emptiness confronted us. Dorothy was not in the little chamber. With an impulsive gesture Sinclair pointed to the bed—it had not been lain in; then to the gas—it was still burning. The communicating room, in which Mrs. Lansing slept, was also lighted, but silent as the one in which we stood. This last struck us as the most incomprehensible fact of all. Mrs. Lansing was not the woman to sleep through a disturbance. Where was she, then? and why did we not hear her strident and aggressive tones rising in angry remonstrance at our intrusion? Had she followed her niece from the room? Should we in another minute encounter her ponderous figure in the group of people we could now hear hurrying toward us? I was for retreating and hunting the house over for Dorothy. But Sinclair, with truer instinct, drew me across the threshold of this silent room.

Well was it for us that we entered there together, for I do not know how either of us, weakened as we were by our forebodings and all the alarms of this unprecedented night, could have borne alone the sight that awaited us.

On the bed situated at the right of the doorway lay a form—awful, ghastly, and unspeakably repulsive. The head, which lay high but inert upon the pillow, was surrounded with the gray hairs of age, and the eyes, which seemed to stare into ours, were glassy with reflected light and not with inward intelligence. This glassiness told the tale of the room's grim silence. It was death we looked on; not the death we had anticipated and for which we were in a measure prepared, but one fully as awful, and having for its victim not Dorothy Camerden nor even Gilbertine Murray, but the heartless aunt, who had driven them both like slaves, and who now lay facing the reward of her earthly deeds, *alone*.

As a realization of the awful truth came upon me, I stumbled against the bedpost, looking on with almost blind eyes as Sinclair bent over the rapidly whitening face, whose naturally ruddy color no one had ever before seen disturbed. And I was still standing there when Mr. Armstrong and all the others came pouring in. Nor have I any distinct remembrance of what was said or how I came to be in the ante-chamber again. All thought, all consciousness even, seemed to forsake me, and I did not really waken to my surroundings till some one near me whispered:

"Apoplexy!"

Then I began to look about me and peer into the faces crowding up on every side, for the only one which could give me back my self-possession. But though there were many girlish countenances to be seen in the awestruck groups huddled in every corner, I beheld no Dorothy, and was therefore but little astonished when in another moment I heard the cry go up:

"Where is Dorothy? Where was she when her aunt died?"

Alas! there was no one there to answer, and the looks of those about, which hitherto had expressed little save awe and fright, turned to wonder, and more than one person left the room as if to look for her. I did not join them. I was rooted to the place. Nor did Sinclair stir a foot, though his eye, which had been wandering restlessly over the faces about him, now settled inquiringly on the doorway. For whom was he looking? Gilbertine or Dorothy? Gilbertine, no doubt, for he visibly brightened as her figure presently appeared clad in a *negligée*, which emphasized her height and gave to her whole appearance a womanly sobriety unusual to it.

She had evidently been told what had occurred, for she asked no questions, only leaned in still horror against the door-post, with her eyes fixed on the room within. Sinclair, advancing, held out his arm. She gave no sign of seeing it. Then he spoke. This seemed to rouse her, for she gave him a grateful look, though she did not take his arm.

"There will be no wedding to-morrow," fell from her lips in self-communing murmur.

Only a few minutes had passed since they had started to find Dorothy, but it seemed an age to me. My body remained in the room, but my mind was searching the house for the girl I loved. Where was she hidden? Would she be found huddled but alive in some far-off chamber? Or was another and more dreadful tragedy awaiting us? I wondered that I could not join the search. I wondered that even Gilbertine's presence could keep Sinclair from doing so. Didn't he know what, in all probability, this missing girl had with her? Didn't he know what I had suffered, was suffering—ah, what now? She is coming! I can hear them speaking to her. Gilbertine moves from the door, and a young man and woman enter with Dorothy between them.

But what a Dorothy! Years could have made no greater change in her. She looked and she moved like one who is done with life, yet fears the few remaining moments left her. Instinctively we fell back before her; instinctively we followed her with our eyes as, reeling a little at the door, she cast a look of inconceivable shrinking, first at her own bed, then at the group of older people watching her with serious looks from the room beyond. As she did so I noted that she was still clad in her evening dress of gray, and that there was no more color on cheek or lip than in the neutral tints of her gown.

Was it our consciousness of the relief which Mrs. Lansing's death, horrible as it was, must bring to this unhappy girl and of the inappropriateness of any display of grief on her part, which caused the silence with which we saw her pass with forced step and dread anticipation into the room where that image of dead virulence awaited her? Impossible to tell. I could not read my own thoughts. How, then, the thoughts of others!

But thoughts, if we had any, all fled when, after one slow turn of her head toward the bed, this trembling young girl gave a choking shriek and fell, face down, on the floor. Evidently she had not been prepared for the look which made her aunt's still face so horrible. How could she have been? Had it not imprinted itself upon my mind as the one revolting vision of my life? How, then, if this young and tender-hearted girl had been insensible to it! As her form struck the floor Mr. Armstrong rushed forward; I had not the right. But it was not by his arms she was lifted. Sinclair was before him, and it was with a singularly determined look I could not understand and which made us all fall back, that he raised her and carried her in to her own bed, where he laid her gently down. Then, as if not content with this simple attention, he hovered over her for a moment arranging the pillows and smoothing her disheveled hair. When at last he left her, the women rushed forward.

"Not too many of you," was his final adjuration, as, giving me a look, he slipped out into the hall.

I followed him immediately. He had gained the moon-lighted corridor near his own door, where he stood awaiting me with something in his hand. As I approached, he drew me to the window and showed me what it was. It was the amethyst box, open and empty, and beside it, shining with a yellow instead of a purple light, the little vial void of the one drop which used to sparkle within it.

"I found the vial in the bed with the old woman," said he. "The box I saw glittering among Dorothy's locks before she fell. That was why I lifted her."

V

THREE O'CLOCK IN THE MORNING

As he spoke, youth with its brilliant hopes, illusions and beliefs passed from me, never to return in the same measure again. I stared at the glimmering amethyst, I stared at the empty vial and, as a full realization of all his words implied seized my benumbed faculties, I felt the icy chill of some grisly horror moving among the roots of my hair, lifting it on my forehead and filling my whole being with shrinking and dismay.

Sinclair, with a quick movement, replaced the tiny flask in its old receptacle, and then thrusting the whole out of sight, seized my hand and wrung it.

"I am your friend," he whispered. "Remember, under all circumstances and in every exigency, your friend."

"What are you going to do with *those*?" I demanded when I regained control of my speech.

"I do not know."

"What are you going to do with—with Dorothy?"

He drooped his head; I could see his fingers working in the moonlight.

"The physicians will soon be here. I heard the telephone going a few minutes ago. When they have pronounced the old woman dead we will give the—the lady you mention an opportunity to explain herself."

Explain herself, she! Simple expectation. Unconsciously I shook my head.

"It is the least we can do," he gently persisted. "Come, we must not be seen with our heads together—not yet. I am sorry that we two were found more or less dressed at the time of the alarm. It may cause comment."

"She was dressed, too," I murmured, as much to myself as to him.

"Unfortunately, yes," was the muttered reply, with which he drew off and hastened into the hall, where the now thoroughly-aroused household stood in a great group about the excited hostess.

Mrs. Armstrong was not the woman for an emergency. With streaming hair and tightly-clutched kimono, she was gesticulating wildly and bemoaning the break in the festivities which this event must necessarily cause. As Sinclair approached, she turned her tirade on him, and as all stood still to listen and add such words of sympathy or disappointment as suggested themselves in the excitement of the moment, I had an opportunity to note that neither of the two girls most interested was within sight. This troubled me. Drawing up to the outside of the circle, I asked Beaton, who was nearest to me, if he knew how Miss Camerden was.

"Better, I hear. Poor girl, it was a great shock to her."

I ventured nothing more. The conventionality of his tone was not to be mistaken. Our conversation on the veranda was to be ignored. I did not know whether to feel relief at this or an added distress. I was in a whirl of emotion which robbed me of all discrimination. As I realized my own condition, I concluded that my wisest move would be to withdraw myself for a time from every eye. Accordingly, and at the risk of offending more than one pretty girl who still had something to say concerning this terrible mischance, I slid away to my room, happy to escape the murmurs and snatches of talk rising on every side. One bitter speech, uttered by I do not know whom, rang in my ears and made all thinking unendurable. It was this:

"Poor woman! she was angry once too often. I heard her scolding Dorothy again after she went to her room. That is why Dorothy is so overcome. She says it was the violence of her aunt's rage which killed her,—a rage of which she unfortunately was the cause."

So there were words again between these two after the door closed upon them for the night! Was this what we heard just before that scream went up? It would seem so. Thereupon, quite against my will, I found myself thinking of Dorothy's changed position before the world. Only yesterday a dependent slave; to-day, the owner of millions. Gilbertine would have her share, a large one, but there was enough to make them both wealthy. Intolerable thought! Would that no money had been involved! I hated to think of those diamonds and—

Oh, anything was better than this! Dashing from my room I joined one of the groups into which the single large circle had now broken up. The house had been lighted from end to end, and some effort had been made at a more respectable appearance by such persons as I now saw; some even were fully dressed. All were engaged in discussing the one great topic. Listening and not listening, I waited for the front door bell to ring. It sounded while one woman was saying to another:

"The Sinclairs will now be able to take their honeymoon on their own yacht."

I made my way to where I could watch Sinclair while the physicians were in the room. I thought his face looked very noble. The narrowness of his own escape, the sympathy for me which the event, so much worse than either of us anticipated, had awakened in his generous breast, had called out all that was best in his naturally reserved and not-always-to-be-understood nature. A tower of strength he was to me that hour. I knew that mercy and mercy only would influence his conduct. He would be guilty of no rash or inconsiderate act. He would give this young girl a chance.

Therefore when the physicians had pronounced the case one of apoplexy (a conclusion most natural under the circumstances), and the excitement which had held together the various groups of uneasy guests had begun to subside, it was with perfect confidence I saw him approach and address Gilbertine. She was standing fully dressed at the stairhead, where she had stopped to hold some conversation with the retiring physicians; and the look she gave him in return and the way she moved off in obedience to his command or suggestion assured me that he was laying plans for an interview with Dorothy. Consequently I was quite ready to obey him when he finally stepped up to me and said:

"Go below, and if you find the library empty, as I have no doubt you will, light one gas-jet and see that the door to the conservatory is unlocked. I require a place in which to make Gilbertine comfortable while I have some words with her cousin."

"But how will you be able to influence Miss Camerden to come down?" Somehow, the familiar name of Dorothy would not pass my lips. "Do you think she will recognize your right to summon her to an interview?"

"Yes."

I had never seen his lip take that firm line before, yet I had always known him to be a man of great resolution.

"But how can you reach her? She is shut up in her own room, under the care, I am told, of Mrs. Armstrong's maid."

"I know, but she will escape that dreadful place as soon as her feet will carry her. I shall wait in the hall till she is seen to enter it, then I will say 'Come!' and she will come, attended by Gilbertine."

"And I? Do you mean me to be present at an interview so painful, nay, so serious and so threatening? It would cut short every word you hope to hear. I—cannot—"

"I have not asked you to. It is imperative that I should see Miss Camerden alone." (He could not call her Dorothy, either.) "I shall ask Gilbertine to accompany us, so that appearances may be preserved. I want you to be able to inform any one who approaches the door that you saw me go in there with Miss Murray."

"Then I am to stay in the hall?"

"If you will be so kind."

The clock struck three.

"It is very late," I exclaimed. "Why not wait till morning?"

"And have the whole house about our ears? No. Besides, some things will not keep an hour, a moment. I must hear what this young girl has to say in response to my questions. Remember, I am the owner of the flask whose contents killed the old woman!"

"You believe she died from swallowing that drop?"

"Absolutely."

I said no more, but hastened down stairs to do his bidding.

I found the lower hall partly lighted, but none of the rooms.

Entering the library, I lit the gas as Sinclair had requested. Then I tried the conservatory door. It was unlocked. Casting a sharp glance around, I made sure that the lounges were all unoccupied and that I could safely leave Sinclair to hold his contemplated interview without fear of interruption. Then, dreading a premature arrival on his part, I slid quickly out and moved down the hall to where the light of the one burning jet failed to penetrate. "I will watch from here," thought I, and entered upon the quick pacing of the floor which my impatience and the overwrought condition of my nerves demanded.

But before I had turned on my steps more than half a dozen times, the single but brilliant ray coming from some half-open door in the rear caught my eye, and I had the curiosity to step back and see if any one was sharing my watch. In doing so I came upon the little spiral staircase which, earlier in the evening, Sinclair had heard creak under some unknown footstep. Had this footstep been Dorothy's, and if so, what had brought her into this remote portion of the house? Fear? Anguish? Remorse? A flying from herself or from *it*? I wished I knew just where she had been found by the two young persons who had brought her back into her aunt's room. No one had volunteered the information, and I had not seen the moment when I felt myself in a position to demand it.

Proceeding further, I stood amazed at my own forgetfulness. The light which had attracted my attention came from the room devoted to the display of Miss Murray's wedding-gifts. This I should have known instantly, having had a hand in their arrangement. But all my faculties were dulled that night, save such as responded to dread and horror. Before going back I paused to look at the detective whose business it was to guard the room. He was sitting very quietly at his post, and if he saw me he did not look up. Strange that I had forgotten this man when keeping my own vigil above. I doubted if Sinclair had remembered him either. Yet he must have been unconsciously sharing our watch from start to finish; must even have heard the cry as only a waking man could hear it. Should I ask him if this was so? No. Perhaps I had not the courage to hear his answer.

Shortly after my return into the main hall I heard steps on the grand staircase. Looking up, I saw the two girls descending, followed by Sinclair. He had been successful, then, in inducing Dorothy to come down. What would be the result? Could I stand the suspense of the impending interview?

As they stepped within the rays of the solitary gas-jet already mentioned, I cast one quick look into Gilbertine's face, then a long one into Dorothy's. I could read neither. If it was horror and horror only which rendered both so pale and fixed of feature, then their emotion was similar in character and intensity. But if in either breast the one dominant sentiment was fear—horrible, blood-curdling fear—then was that fear confined to Dorothy; for while Gilbertine advanced bravely, Dorothy's steps lagged, and at the point where she should have turned into the library, she whirled sharply about and made as if she would fly back up stairs.

But one stare from Gilbertine, one word from Sinclair, recalled her to herself and she passed in and the door closed upon the three. I was left to prevent possible intrusion and to eat out my heart in intolerable suspense.

VI

DOROTHY SPEAKS

I shall not subject you to the ordeal from which I suffered. You shall follow my three friends into the room. According to Sinclair's description, the interview proceeded thus:

As soon as the door had closed upon them, and before either of the girls had a chance to speak, he remarked to Gilbertine:

"I have brought you here because I wish to express to you, in the presence of your cousin, my sympathy for the bereavement which in an instant has robbed you both of a lifelong guardian. I also wish to say in the light of this sad event, that I am ready, if propriety so exacts, to postpone the ceremony which I hoped would unite our lives to-day. Your wish shall be my wish, Gilbertine; though I would suggest that possibly you never more needed the sympathy and protection which only a husband can give than you do to-day."

He told me afterward that he was so taken up with the effect of this suggestion on Gilbertine that he forgot to look at Dorothy, though the hint he strove to convey of impending trouble was meant as much for her as for his affianced bride. In another moment he regretted this, especially when he saw that Dorothy had changed her attitude and was now looking away from them both.

"What do you say, Gilbertine?" he asked earnestly, as she sat flushing and paling before him.

"Nothing. I have not thought—it is a question for others to decide—others who know what is right better than I. I appreciate your consideration," she suddenly burst out—"and should be glad to tell you at this moment what to expect; but—give me a little time—let me see you later—in the morning, Mr. Sinclair, after we are all somewhat rested and when I can see you quite alone."

Dorothy rose.

"Shall I go?" she asked.

Sinclair advanced and with quiet protest, touched her on the shoulder. Quietly she sank back into her seat.

"I want to say a half-dozen words to you, Miss Camerden. Gilbertine will pardon us; it is about matters which must be settled to-night. There are decisions to arrive at and arrangements to be made. Mrs. Armstrong has instructed me to question you in regard to these, as the one best acquainted with Mrs. Lansing's affairs and general tastes. We will not trouble Gilbertine. She has her own decisions to reach. Dear, will you let me make you comfortable in the conservatory while I talk for five minutes with Dorothy?"

He said she met this question with a look so blank and uncomprehending that he just lifted her and carried her in among the palms.

"I must speak to Dorothy," he pleaded, placing her in the chair where he had often seen her sit of her own accord. "Be a good girl; I will not keep you here long."

"But why can not I go to my room? I do not understand—I am frightened— what have you to say to Dorothy you can not say to me?"

She seemed so excited that for a minute, just a minute, he faltered in his purpose. Then he took her gravely by the hand.

"I have told you," said he. Then he kissed her softly on the forehead. "Be quiet, dear, and rest. See! here are roses."

He plucked and flung a handful into her lap. Then he crossed back to the library and shut the conservatory door behind him. I am not surprised that Gilbertine wondered at her peremptory bridegroom.

When Sinclair reëntered the library, he found Dorothy standing with her hand on the knob of the door leading into the hall. Her head was bent and thoughtful, as though she were inwardly debating whether to stand her ground or fly. Sinclair gave her no further opportunity for hesitation. Advancing rapidly, he laid his hand quietly on hers, and with a gravity which must have impressed her, quietly remarked:

"I must ask you to stay and hear what I have to say. I wished to spare Gilbertine; would that I could spare you. But circumstances forbid. You know and I know that your aunt did not die of apoplexy."

She gave a violent start and her lips parted. If the hand under his clasp had been cold, it was now icy. He let his own slip from the contact.

"You know!" she echoed, trembling and pallid, her released hand flying instinctively to her hair.

"Yes; you need not feel about for the little box. I took it from its hiding-place when I laid you fainting on the bed. Here it is."

He drew it from his pocket and showed it to her. She hardly glanced at it; her eyes were fixed in terror on his face and her lips seemed to be trying in vain to formulate some inquiry.

He tried to be merciful.

"I missed it many hours ago, from the shelf yonder where you all saw me place it. Had I known that you had taken it, I would have repeated to you how deadly were the contents, and how dangerous it was to handle the vial or to let others handle it, much less to put it to the lips."

She started and instinctively her form rose to its full height.

"Have you looked in that little box since you took it from my hair?" she asked.

"Yes."

"Then you know it to be empty."

For answer he pressed the spring, and the little lid flew open.

"It is not empty now, you see." Then more slowly and with infinite meaning, "But the little flask is."

She brought her hands together and faced him with a noble dignity which at once put the interview on a different footing.

"Where was this vial found?" she demanded.

He found it difficult to answer. They seemed to have exchanged positions. When he did speak it was in a low tone and with less confidence than he had shown before.

"In the bed with the old lady. I saw it there myself. Mr. Worthington was with me. Nobody else knows anything about it. I wished to give you an opportunity to explain. I begin to think you can—but how, God only knows. The box was hidden in your hair from early evening. I saw your hand continually fluttering toward it all the time we were dancing in the parlor."

She did not lose an iota of her dignity or pride.

"You are right," she said. "I put it there as soon as I took it from the cabinet. I could think of no safer hiding-place. Yes, I took it," she acknowledged as she saw the flush rise to his cheek. "I took it; but with no worse motive than the dishonest one of having for my own an object which bewitched me; I was hardly myself when I snatched it from the shelf and thrust it into my hair."

He stared at her in amazement, her confession and her attitude so completely contradicted each other.

"But I had nothing to do with the vial," she went on. And with this declaration her whole manner, even her voice changed, as if with the utterance of these few words she had satisfied some inner demand of self-respect and could now enter into the sufferings of those about her. "This I think it right to make plain to you. I supposed the vial to be in the box when I took it, but when I got to my room and had an opportunity to examine the deadly trinket, I found it empty, just as you found it when you took it from my hair. Some one had taken the vial out before my hand had ever touched the box."

Like a man who feels himself suddenly seized by the throat, yet who struggles for the life slowly but inexorably leaving him, Sinclair cast one heartrending look toward the conservatory, then heavily demanded:

"Why were you out of your room? Why did they have to look for you? *And who was the person who uttered that scream?*"

She confronted him sadly, but with an earnestness he could not but respect.

"I was not in the room because I was troubled by my discovery. I think I had some idea of returning the box to the shelf from which I had taken it. At all events, I found myself on the little staircase in the rear when that cry rang through the house. I do not know who uttered it; I only know that it did not spring from my lips."

In a rush of renewed hope he seized her by the hand.

"It was your aunt!" he whispered. "It was she who took the vial out of the box; who put it to her own lips; who shrieked when she felt her vitals gripped. Had you stayed you would have known this. Can't you say so? Don't you think so? Why do you look at me with those incredulous eyes?"

"Because you must not believe a lie. Because you are too good a man to be sacrificed. It was a younger throat than my aunt's which gave utterance to that shriek. Mr. Sinclair, be advised; *do not be married to-morrow!*"

Meanwhile I was pacing the hall without in a delirium of suspense. I tried hard to keep within the bounds of silence. I had turned for the fiftieth time to face that library door, when suddenly I heard a hoarse cry break from within and saw the door fly open and Dorothy come hurrying out. She shrank when she saw me, but seemed grateful that I did not attempt to stop her, and soon was up the stairs and out of sight. I rushed at once into the library.

I found Sinclair sitting before a table with his head buried in his hands. In an instant I knew that our positions were again reversed and, without stopping to give heed to my own sensations, I approached him as near as I dared and laid my hand on his shoulder.

He shuddered but did not look up, and it was minutes before he spoke. Then it all came in a rush.

"Fool! fool that I was! And I saw that she was consumed by fright the moment it became plain that I was intent upon having some conversation with Dorothy. Her fingers where they gripped my arm must have left marks behind them. But I saw only womanly nervousness where a man less blind would have detected guilt. Walter, I wish that the mere scent of this empty flask would kill. Then I should not have to reënter that conservatory door—or look again in her face, or—"

He had taken out the cursed jewel and was fingering it in a nervous way which went to my heart of hearts. Gently removing it from his hand, I asked with all the calmness possible:

"What is all this mystery? Why have your suspicions returned to Gilbertine? I thought you had entirely dissociated her with this matter and that you blamed Dorothy and Dorothy only, for the amethyst's loss?"

"Dorothy had the empty box; but the vial! the vial!—that had been taken by a previous hand. Do you remember the white silk train which Mr. Armstrong saw slipping from this room? I can not talk, Walter; my duty leads me *there.*"

He pointed toward the conservatory. I drew back and asked if I should take up my watch again outside the door.

He shook his head.

"It makes no difference; nothing makes any difference. But if you want to please me, stay here."

I at once sank into a chair. He made a great effort and advanced to the conservatory door. I studiously looked another way; my heart was breaking with sympathy for him.

But in another instant I was on my feet. I could hear him rushing about among the palms. Presently I heard his voice shout out the wild cry:

"She is gone! I forgot there was another door communicating with the hall."

I crossed the floor and entered where he stood gazing down at an empty seat and a trail of scattered roses. Never shall I forget his face. The dimness of the spot could not hide his deep, unspeakable emotions. To him this flight bore but one interpretation—guilt.

I did not advocate Sinclair's pressing the matter further that night. I saw that he was exhausted and that any further movement would tax him beyond his strength. We therefore separated immediately after leaving the library, and I found my way to my own room alone. It may seem callous in me, but I fell asleep very soon after, and did not wake till roused by a knock at my door. On opening it I confronted Sinclair, looking haggard and unkempt. As he entered, the first clear notes of the breakfast-bell could be heard rising up from the lower hall.

"I have not slept," he said. "I have been walking the hall all night, listening by spells at her door, and at other times giving what counsel I could to the Armstrongs. God forgive me, but I have said nothing to any one of what has made this affair an awful tragedy to me! Do you think I did wrong? I waited to give Dorothy a chance. Why should I not show the same consideration to Gilbertine?"

"You should." But our eyes did not meet, and neither voice expressed the least hope.

"I shall not go to breakfast," he now declared. "I have written this line to Gilbertine. Will you see that she gets it?"

For reply I held out my hand. He placed the note in it, and I was touched to see that it was unsealed.

"Be sure, when you give it to her, that she will have an opportunity of reading it alone. I shall request the use of one of the little reception-rooms this morning. Let her come there if she is so impelled. She will find a friend as well as a judge."

I endeavored to express sympathy, urge patience and suggest hope. But he had no ear for words, though he tried to listen, poor fellow! so I soon stopped and he presently left the room. I immediately made myself as presentable as a night of unprecedented emotions would allow, and went below to do him such service as opportunity offered and the exigencies of the case permitted.

I found the lower hall alive with eager guests and a few outsiders. News of the sad event was slowly making its way through the avenue, and some of the Armstrongs' nearest neighbors had left their breakfast-tables to express their interest and to hear the particulars. Among these stood the lady of the house; but Mr.

Armstrong was nowhere within sight. For him the breakfast waited. Not wishing to be caught in any little swirl of conventional comment, I remained near the staircase waiting for some one to descend who could give me news concerning Miss Murray. For I had small expectation of her braving the eyes of these strangers, and doubted if even Dorothy would be seen at the breakfast-table. But little Miss Lane, if small, was gifted with a great appetite. She would be sure to appear prior to the last summons, and as we were good friends, she would listen to my questions and give me the answer I needed for the carrying out of Sinclair's wishes. But before her light footfall was heard descending I was lured from my plans by an unexpected series of events. Three men came down, one after the other, followed by Mr. Armstrong, looking even more grave and ponderous than usual. Two of them were the physicians who had been called in the night and whom I had myself seen depart somewhere near three o'clock. The third I did not know, but he looked like a doctor also. Why were they here again so early? Had anything new come to light?

It was a question which seemed to strike others as well as myself. As Mr. Armstrong ushered them down the hall and out of the front door, many were the curious glances which followed them, and it was with difficulty that the courteous host on his return escaped the questions and detaining hands of some of his more inquisitive guests. A pleasant word, an amiable smile he had for all, but I was quite certain when I saw him disappear into the little room he retained for his own use that he had told them nothing which could in any way relieve their curiosity.

This filled me with a vague alarm. Something must have occurred—something which Sinclair ought to know. I felt a great anxiety and was closely watching the door behind which Mr. Armstrong had vanished when it suddenly opened and I perceived that he had been writing a telegram. As he gave it to one of the servants he made a gesture to the man standing with extended hand by the Chinese gong, and the summons rang out for breakfast. Instantly the hum of voices ceased, and young and old turned toward the dining-room, but the host did not enter with them. Before the younger and more active of his guests could reach his side he had slid into the room which I have before described as set apart for the display of Gilbertine's wedding-presents. Instantly I lost all inclination for breakfast and lingered about in the hall until every one had passed me, even little Miss Lane, who had come down unperceived while I was watching Mr. Armstrong's door. Not very well pleased with myself for having missed the one opportunity which might have been of service to me, I was asking myself whether I should follow her and make the best attempt I could at sociability if not at eating, when Mr. Armstrong approached from the side hall, and, accosting me, inquired if Mr. Sinclair had come down yet.

I assured him that I had not seen him and did not think he meant to come to breakfast, adding that he had been very much affected by the affairs of the night, and had told me that he was going to shut himself up in his room and rest.

"I am sorry, but there is a question I must ask him immediately. It is about a little Italian trinket which I am told he displayed to the ladies yesterday afternoon."

VII

CONSTRAINT

So! our dreadful secret was not confined to ourselves as we had supposed, but was shared or at least suspected, by our host.

Thankful that it was I, rather than Sinclair, who was called upon to meet and sustain this shock, I answered with what calmness I could:

"Yes; Sinclair mentioned the matter to me. Indeed, if you have any curiosity on the subject, I think I can enlighten you as fully as he can."

Mr. Armstrong glanced up the stairs, hesitated, then drew me into his private room.

"I find myself in a very uncomfortable position," he began. "A strange and quite unaccountable change has shown itself in the appearance of Mrs. Lansing's body during the last few hours; a change which baffles the physicians and raises in their minds very unfortunate conjectures. What I want to know is whether Mr. Sinclair still has in his possession the box which is said to hold a vial of deadly poison, or whether it has passed into any other hand since he showed it to certain ladies in the library."

We were standing directly in the light of an eastern window. Deception was impossible, even if I had felt like employing it. In Sinclair's interests, if not in my own, I resolved to be as true to our host as our positions demanded, yet, at the same time, to save Gilbertine as much as possible from premature if not final suspicion.

I therefore replied: "That is a question I can answer as well as Sinclair." (Happy was I to save him this cross-examination.) "While he was showing this toy, Mrs. Armstrong came into the room and proposed a stroll, which drew all of the ladies from the room and called for his attendance as well. With no thought of the danger involved, he placed the trinket on a high shelf in the cabinet, and went out with the rest. When he came back for it, it was gone."

The usually ruddy aspect of my host's face deepened, and he sat down in the great armchair which did duty before his writing-table.

"This is dreadful," was his comment, "entailing I do not know what unfortunate consequences upon this household and on the unhappy girl—"

"Girl?" I repeated.

He turned upon me with great gravity. "Mr. Worthington, I am sorry to have to admit it, but something strange, something not easily explainable, took place in this house last night. It has only just come to light; otherwise, the doctors' conclusions might have been different. You know there is a detective in the house. The presents are valuable and I thought best to have a man here to look after them."

I nodded; I had no breath for speech.

"That man tells me," continued Mr. Armstrong, "that just a few minutes previous to the time the whole household was aroused last night, he heard a step in the hall overhead, then the sound of a light foot descending the little staircase in the servants' hall. Being anxious to find out what this person wanted at an hour so late, he lowered the gas, closed his door and listened. The steps went by his door. Satisfied that it was a woman he heard, he pulled open the door again and looked out. A young girl was standing not very far from him in a thin streak of moonlight. She was gazing intently at something in her hand, and that something had a purple gleam to it. He is ready to swear to this. Next moment, frightened by some noise she heard, she fled back and vanished again in the region of the little staircase. It was soon, very soon after this that the shriek came. Now, Mr. Worthington, what am I to do with this knowledge? I have advised this man to hold his peace till I can make inquiries, but where am I to make them? I can not think that Miss Camerden—"

The ejaculation which escaped me was involuntary. To hear her name for the second time in this association was more than I could bear.

"Did he say it was Miss Camerden?" I hurriedly inquired as he looked at me in some surprise. "How should he know Miss Camerden?"

"He described her," was the unanswerable reply. "Besides, we know that she was circulating in the halls at that time. I declare I have never known a worse business," this amiable man bemoaned. "Let me send for Sinclair; he is more interested than any one else in Gilbertine's relatives; or stay, what if I should send for Miss Camerden herself? She should be able to tell how she came by this box."

I subdued my own instincts, which were all for clearing Dorothy on the spot, and answered as I thought Sinclair would like me to answer.

"It is a serious and very perplexing piece of business," said I; "but if you will wait a short time I do not think you will have to trouble Miss Camerden. I am sure that explanations will be given. Give the lady a chance," I stammered. "Imagine what her feelings would be if questioned on so delicate a topic. It would make a breach which nothing could heal. Later, if she does not speak, it will be only right for you to ask her why."

"She did not come down this morning."

"Naturally not."

"If I could take counsel of my wife! But she is of too nervous a temperament. I am anxious to keep her from knowing this fresh complication as long as possible. Do you think I can look for Miss Camerden to explain herself before the doctors return, or before Mrs. Lansing's physician, for whom I have telegraphed, can arrive from New York?"

"I am sure that three hours will not pass before you hear the truth. Leave me to work out the situation. I promise that if I can not bring it about to your satisfaction, Sinclair shall be asked to lend his assistance. Only keep the gossips from Miss Camerden's good name. Words can be said in a moment that will not be forgotten in years. I tremble at such a prospect for her."

"No one knows of her being seen with the box," he remarked. "Every one probably knows by this time that there is some doubt felt as to the cause of Mrs. Lansing's death. You can not keep a suspicion of this nature secret in a house so full of people as this."

I knew it, but, relieved by his manner if not by his words, I took my leave of him for the present and made my way at once to the dining-room. Should I find Miss Lane there? Yes, and what was more, the fortunes of the day had decreed that the place beside her should be unoccupied.

I was on my way to that place when I was struck by the extreme quiet into which the room had fallen. It had been humming with talk when I first entered; but now not a voice was raised, and scarcely an eye. In the hurried glance I cast about the board, not a look met mine in recognition or welcome.

What did it mean? Had they been talking about me? Possibly; and in a way, it would seem, that was not altogether flattering to my vanity.

Unable to hide my sense of the general embarrassment which my presence had called forth, I passed to the seat I have indicated and let my inquiring look settle on Miss Lane. She was staring in imitation of the others straight into her plate, but as I saluted her with a quiet good morning, she looked up and acknowledged my courtesy with a faint, almost sympathetic, smile. At once the whole tableful broke again into chatter, and I could safely put the question with which my mind was full.

"How is Miss Murray?" I asked. "I do not see her here."

"Did you expect to? Poor Gilbertine! This is not the bridal day she expected." Then, with irresistible naïveté entirely in keeping with her fairy-like figure and girlish face, she added: "I think it was just horrid in the old woman to die the night before the wedding; don't you?"

"Indeed, I do," I emphatically rejoined, humoring her in the hope of learning what I wished to know. "Does Miss Murray still cherish the expectation of being married to-day? No one seems to know."

"Nor do I. I haven't seen her since the middle of the night. She didn't come back to her room. They say she is sobbing out her terror and disappointment in some attic corner. Think of that for Gilbertine Murray! But even that is better than—"

The sentence trailed away into an indistinguishable murmur; the murmur into silence. Was it because of a fresh lull in the conversation about us? I hardly think so, for though the talk was presently resumed, she remained silent, not even giving the least sign of wishing to prolong this particular topic. I finished my coffee as soon as possible and quitted the room, but not before many had preceded me.

The hall was consequently as full as before of a gossiping crowd.

I was on the point of bowing myself through the various groups blocking my way to the library door, when I noticed renewed signs of embarrassment on all the faces turned my way. Women who were clustered about the newel-post drew back, and some others sauntered away into side rooms with an appearance of suddenly wishing to go somewhere. This certainly was very singular, especially as these marks of disapproval did not seem to be directed so much at myself as at some one behind me. Who could this some one be? Turning quickly, I cast a glance up the staircase before which I stood and saw the figure of a young girl dressed in black hesitating on the landing. This young girl was Dorothy Camerden, and it took but a moment's contemplation of the scene for me to feel assured that it was against her this feeling of universal constraint had been directed.

VIII

GILBERTINE SPEAKS

Knowing my darling's innocence, I felt the insult shown her in my heart of hearts, and might in the heat of the moment have been betrayed into an unwise utterance of my indignation, if at that moment I had not encountered the eye of Mr. Armstrong, fixed on me from the rear hall. In the mingled surprise and distress he displayed, I saw that it was not from any indiscretion of his that this feeling against her had started. He had not betrayed the trust I had placed in him, yet the murmur had gone about which virtually ostracized her, and instead of confronting the eager looks of friends, she found herself met by averted glances and coldly turned backs, and soon by an almost empty hall.

She flushed as she realized the effect of her presence and cast me an agonized look, which, without her expectation, perhaps, roused every instinct of chivalry within me. Advancing, I met her at the foot of the stairs, and with one quick word seemed to restore her to herself.

"Be patient!" I whispered. "To-morrow they will be all around you again. Perhaps sooner. Go into the conservatory and wait."

She gave me a grateful pressure of the hand, while I bounded up stairs, determined that nothing should stop me from finding Gilbertine and giving her the letter with which Sinclair had intrusted me.

But this was more easily planned than accomplished. When I had reached the third floor (an unaccustomed and strange spot for me to find myself in) I at first found no one who could tell me to which room Miss Murray had retired. Then, when I did come across a stray housemaid and she, with an extraordinary stare, had pointed out the door, I found it quite impossible to gain any response from within, though I could hear a quick step moving restlessly to and fro and now and then catch the sound of a smothered sob or low cry. The wretched girl would not heed me, though I told her who I was and that I had a letter from Mr. Sinclair in my hand. Indeed, she presently became perfectly quiet and let me knock again and again, till the situation became ridiculous and I felt obliged to draw off.

Not that I thought of yielding. No, I would stay there till her own fancy drove her to open the door, or till Mr. Armstrong should come up and force it. A woman upon whom so many interests depended would not be allowed to remain shut up the whole morning. Her position as a possible bride forbade it. Guilty or innocent, she must show herself before long. As if in answer to my expectation, a figure appeared at this very moment at the other end of the hall. It was Dutton, the butler, and in his hand he held a telegram. He seemed astonished to see me there, but passed me with a simple bow and stopped before the door I had so unavailingly assailed a few minutes before.

"A telegram, miss," he shouted, as no answer was made to his knock. "Mr. Armstrong asked me to bring it to you. It is from the bishop and calls for an immediate reply."

There was a stir within, but the door did not open. Meanwhile, I had sealed and thrust forth the letter I had held concealed in my breast pocket.

"Give her this, too," I signified, and pointed to the crack under the door.

He took the letter, laid the telegram on it, and pushed them both in. Then he stood up and eyed the unresponsive panels with the set look of a man who does not easily yield his purpose.

"I will wait for the answer," he shouted through the keyhole, and falling back he took up his stand against the opposite wall.

I could not keep him company there. Withdrawing into a big dormer window, I waited with beating heart to see if her door would open. Apparently not, yet as I still lingered, I heard the lock turn, followed by the sound of a measured but hurried step. Dashing from my retreat, I reached the main hall in time to see Miss Murray disappear toward the staircase. This was well, and I was about to follow when, to my astonishment, I perceived Dutton standing in the doorway she had just left, staring down at the floor with a puzzled look.

"She didn't pick up the letters," he cried, in amazement. "She just walked over them. What shall I do now? It's the strangest thing I ever saw."

"Take them to the little boudoir over the porch," I suggested. "Mr. Sinclair is there and if she is not on her way to join him now she certainly will be soon."

Without a word Dutton caught up the letters and made for the stairs.

Left to await the result, I found myself so worked upon that I wondered how much longer I should find myself able to endure these shifts of feeling and constantly recurring moments of extreme suspense. To escape the torture of my own thoughts, or, possibly, to get some idea of how Dorothy was sustaining an ordeal which was fast destroying my own self-possession, I prepared to go down stairs. What was my astonishment in passing the little boudoir on the second floor, to find its door ajar and the place empty. Either the interview between Sinclair and Gilbertine had been very much curtailed, or it had not yet taken place. With a heart heavy with forebodings I no longer sought to analyze, I made my way down and reached the lower step of the great staircase just as a half-dozen girls, rushing from different quarters of the hall, surrounded the heavy form of Mr. Armstrong coming from his own little room.

Their questions made a small hubbub. With a good-natured gesture, he put them all back and, raising his voice, said to the assembled crowd:

"It has been decided by Miss Murray that, under the circumstances, it will be wiser for her to postpone the celebration of her marriage to some time and place less fraught with mournful suggestions. A telegram has just been sent to the bishop to that effect, and while we all suffer from this disappointment, I am sure there is no one here who will not see the propriety of her decision."

As he finished, Gilbertine appeared behind him. At the same moment I caught, or thought I did, the flash of Sinclair's eye from the recesses of the room beyond; but I could not stop to make sure of this, for Gilbertine's look and manner were such as to draw my full attention, and it was with a mixture of almost inexplicable emotions that I saw her thread her way among her friends, in a state of high feeling which made her blind to their outstretched hands and deaf to the murmur of interest and sympathy which instinctively followed her. She was making for the stairs, and whatever her thoughts, whatever the state of her mind, she moved superbly, in her pale, yet seemingly radiant abstraction. I watched her, fascinated, yet when she left the last group and began to cross the small square of carpet which alone separated us, I stepped down and aside, feeling that to meet her eye just then without knowing what had passed between her and Sinclair would be cruel to her and well-nigh unbearable to myself.

She saw the movement and seemed to hesitate an instant, then she turned for one brief instant in my direction, and I saw her smile. Great God! it was the smile of innocence. Fleeting as it was, the pride that was in it, the sweet assertion and the joy were unmistakable. I felt like springing to Sinclair's side in the gladness of my relief, but there was no time; another door had opened down the hall, another person had stepped upon the scene, and Miss Murray, as well as myself, recognized by the hush which at once fell upon every one present that something of still more startling import awaited us.

"Mr. Armstrong and ladies!" said this stranger (I knew he was a stranger by the studied formality of the former's bow). "I have made a few inquiries since I came here a short time ago, and I find that there is one young lady in the house who ought to be able to tell me better than any one else under what circumstances Mrs. Lansing breathed her last. I allude to her niece, who slept in the adjoining room. Is that young lady here? Her name, if I remember rightly, is Camerden—Miss Dorothy Camerden."

A movement as of denial passed from group to group down the hall, and, while no one glanced toward the library and some did glance up stairs, I felt the dart of sudden fear—or was it hope—that Dorothy, hearing her name called, would leave the conservatory and proudly confront the speaker in face of this whole suspicious throng. But no Dorothy appeared. On the contrary, it was Gilbertine who turned, and with an air of authority for which no one was prepared, asked in tones vibrating with feeling:

"Has this gentleman the official right to question who was and who was not with my aunt when she died?"

Mr. Armstrong, who showed his surprise as ingenuously as he did every other emotion, glanced up at the light figure hovering over them from the staircase and made out to answer:

"This gentleman has every right, Miss Murray. He is the coroner of the town, accustomed to inquire into all cases of sudden death."

"Then," she vehemently rejoined, her pale cheeks breaking out into a scarlet flush, above which her eyes shone with an almost unearthly brilliancy, "do not summon Dorothy Camerden. She is not the witness you want. I am. I am the one who uttered that scream; I am the one who saw our aunt die. Dorothy can not tell you what took place in her room and at her bedside, for Dorothy was not there; but *I* can."

Amazed, not as others were, at the assertion itself, but at the manner and publicity of the utterance, I contemplated this surprising girl in ever-increasing wonder. Always beautiful, always spirited and proud, she looked at that moment as if nothing in the shape of fear, or even contumely, could touch her. She faced the astonishment of her best friends with absolute fearlessness, and before the general murmur could break into words, added:

"I feel it my duty to speak thus publicly, because, by keeping silent so long, I have allowed a false impression to go about. Stunned with terror, I found it impossible to speak during that first shock. Besides, I was in a measure to blame for the catastrophe itself and lacked courage to own it. It was I who took the little crystal flask into my aunt's room. I had been fascinated by it from the first, fascinated enough to long to see it closer and to hold it in my hand. But I was ashamed of this fascination, ashamed, I mean, to have any one know that I could be moved by such a childish impulse; so, instead of taking the box itself, which might easily be missed, I simply abstracted the tiny vial. It strikes me now as a very strange thing for me to do, but then it seemed a natural enough impulse; and it was with a feeling of decided satisfaction I carried this coveted object about with me till I got to my room. Then, when the house was quiet and my room-mate asleep, I took it out and looked at it, and feeling an irresistible desire to share my amusement with my cousin, I stole to her room by means of the connecting balcony, just as I had done many times before when our aunt was in bed and asleep. But unlike any previous occasion, I found the room empty. Dorothy was not there; but as the light was burning high I knew she would soon be back and so ventured to step in. Instantly, I heard my aunt's voice. She was awake and wanted something. She had evidently called before, for her voice was sharp with impatience, and she used some very harsh words. When she heard me in Dorothy's room, she shouted again, and, as I have always been accustomed to obey her commands, I hastened to her side, with the little vial concealed in my hand. As she had expected to see Dorothy and not me, she rose up in unreasoning anger, asking where my cousin was and why I was not in bed. I attempted to answer her, but she would not listen to me and bade me turn up the gas, which I did. Then with her eyes fixed on mine as though she knew I was trying to conceal something from her, she commanded me to rearrange her hair and make her more comfortable. This I could not do with the tiny flask still in my hand, so with a quick movement, which I hoped would pass unobserved, I slid it behind some bottles standing on a table by the bedside, and bent to do what she required. But to attempt to escape her eye was useless. She had seen my action and at once began to feel about for what I had attempted to hide from her. Coming in contact with the tiny flask, she seized it, and with a smile I shall never forget held it up between us. 'What's this?' she cried, showing such astonishment at its minuteness and perfection of shape that it was immediately apparent she had heard nothing of the amethyst box displayed by Mr. Sinclair in the library. 'I never saw a bottle as small as this before. What is in it and why were you so afraid of my seeing it?' As she spoke, she attempted to wrench out the stopper. It stuck, so I was in hopes she would fail in the effort, but she was a woman of uncommon strength and presently it yielded and I saw the vial open in her hand.

"Aghast with terror, I caught at the table beside me, fearing to drop before her eyes. Instantly, her look of curiosity changed to one of suspicion, and repeating, 'What's in it? What's in it?' she raised the flask to her nostrils, and when she found she could make out nothing from the smell, lowered it to her lips, with the intention, I suppose, of determining its contents by tasting them. As I caught sight of this fatal action, and beheld the one drop, which Mr. Sinclair had said was enough to kill a man, slip from its hiding-place of centuries into her open throat, I felt as if the poison had entered my own veins; I could neither speak nor move. But when, an instant later, I met the look which spread suddenly over her face—a look of horror and hatred, accusing horror and unspeakable hatred mingled with what I dimly felt must mean death—an agonized cry burst from my lips, after which, panicstricken, I flew as if for life, back by the way I had come, to my own room. This was a great mistake. I should have remained with my aunt and boldly met the results of the tragedy which my folly had brought about. But terror knows no law, and having once yielded to the instinct of concealment, I knew no other course than to continue to maintain an apparent ignorance of what had just occurred. With chattering teeth and an awful numbness at my heart, I tore off my wrapper and slid into bed. Miss Lane had not wakened, but every one else had and the hall was full of people. This terrified me still more, and for the moment I felt that I could never own the truth and bring down upon myself all this wonder and curiosity. So I allowed a wrong impression of the event to go about, for which act of cowardice I now ask the pardon of every one here, as I have already asked that of Mr. Sinclair and of our kind friend, Mr. Armstrong."

She paused, and stood for a moment confronting us all with proud eyes and flaming cheeks, then amid a hubbub which did not seem to affect her in the least, she stepped down, and approaching the man who, she had been told, had a right to her full confidence, she said, loud enough for all who wished to hear her:

"I am ready to give you whatever further information you may require. Shall I step into the drawing-room with you?"

He bowed and as they disappeared from the great hall the hubbub of voices became tumultuous.

Naturally I should have joined in the universal expressions of surprise and the gossip incident to such an unexpected revelation. But I found myself averse to any kind of talk. Till I could meet Sinclair's eye and discern in it the happy clearing-up of all his doubts, I should not feel free to be my own ordinary and sociable self again. But Sinclair showed every evidence of wishing to keep in the background, and while this was natural enough, so far as people in general were concerned, I thought it odd and very unlike him not to give me an opportunity to express my congratulations at the turn affairs had taken and the frank attitude assumed by Gilbertine. I own I felt much disturbed by this neglect, and as the minutes passed and he failed to appear, I found my satisfaction in her explanations dwindle under the consciousness that they had failed, in some respects, to account for the situation; and before I knew it, I was the prey of fresh doubts which I did my best to smother, not only for the sake of Sinclair, but because I was still too much under the influence of Gilbertine's imposing personality to wish to believe aught but what her burning words conveyed. She must have spoken the truth, but was it the entire truth? I hated myself for asking the question; hated myself for being more critical with her than I had been with Dorothy, who certainly had not made her own part in this tragedy as clear as one who loved her could wish. Ah, Dorothy! it was time some one told her that Gilbertine had openly vindicated her and that she could now come forth and face her friends without hesitation and without dread. Was she still in the conservatory? Doubtless. But it would be better perhaps for me to make sure.

Approaching the place by the small door connecting it with the hall-way in which I stood, I took a hurried look within, and, seeing no one, stepped boldly down between the palms to the little nook where lovers of this quiet spot were accustomed to sit. It was empty, and so was the library beyond. Coming back, I accosted Dutton, whom I found superintending the removal of the potted plants which encumbered the passages, and asked him if he knew where Miss Camerden was? He answered without hesitation that she had stood in the rear hall a little while before, listening to Miss Murray; that she had then gone up stairs by the spiral staircase, leaving word with him that if anybody wanted her she would be found in the small boudoir over the porch.

I thanked him and was on my way to join her, when Mr. Armstrong called me. He must have kept me a half-hour in his room, discussing every aspect of the affair and apologizing for the necessity which he now felt for bidding farewell to most of his guests, among whom, he was careful to state, he did not include me. Then, when I thought this topic exhausted, he began to talk about his wife, and what this dreadful occurrence was to her and how he despaired of ever reconciling her to the fact that it had been considered necessary to call in a coroner. Then he spoke of Sinclair, but with some constraint and a more careful choice of words, at which, realizing that I was to reap nothing from this interview, only suffer strong and continual irritation at a delay which was costing me the inestimable privilege of being the first to tell Dorothy of her reëstablishment in every one's good opinion, I exerted myself for release and to such good purpose that I presently found myself again in the hall, where the first person I ran against was Sinclair.

He started and so did I at this unexpected encounter. Then we stood still, and I stared at him in amazement, for everything about the man was changed, and—inexplicable fact!—in nothing was this change more marked than in his attitude toward myself. Yet he tried to be friendly and meet me on the old footing, and observed as soon as we found ourselves beyond the hearing of others:

"You heard what Gilbertine said. There is no reason for doubting her words.

I do not doubt them and you will show yourself my friend by not doubting them either." Then with some impetuosity and a gleam in his eye quite foreign to its natural expression, he pursued, with a pitiful effort to speak dispassionately: "Our wedding is postponed—indefinitely. There are reasons why this seemed best to Miss Murray. To you, I will say, that postponed nuptials seldom culminate in marriage. In fact, I have just released Miss Murray from all obligations to myself."

The stare of utter astonishment I gave him called up a flush, the first and only one I have ever seen on his face. What was I to say, what could I say, in response to such a declaration, following so immediately upon his warm assertion of her innocence? Nothing. With that indefinable chill between us, which had come I knew not how, I felt tongue-tied.

He saw my embarrassment, possibly my emotion, for he smiled somewhat bitterly and put a step or so between us before he remarked:

"Miss Murray has my good wishes. Out of respect to her position I shall show her a friend's attention while we remain in this house. That is all I have to say, Walter. You and I have held our last conversation on this subject."

He was gone before I had sufficiently recovered to realize that in this conversation I had had no part, neither had it contained any explanation of the very facts which had once formed our greatest grounds for doubt, namely, Beaton's dream, the smothered cry uttered behind Sinclair's shoulder when he first made known the deadly qualities of the little vial, and lastly, the strange desire acknowledged to by both these young ladies to touch and hold an object calculated rather to repel than to attract the normal feminine heart.

At every previous stage of this ever-shifting drama, my instinct had been to set my wits against the facts, and, if I could, puzzle out the mystery. But I felt no such temptation now. My one desire was to act, and that immediately. Dorothy, for all Gilbertine's intimation to the contrary, held the key to the enigma in her own breast. Otherwise, she would not have ventured upon that surprising and necessarily unpalatable advice to Sinclair—an advice he seemed to have followed—not to marry Gilbertine Murray at the time proposed. Nothing, short of a secret acquaintanceship with facts unknown as yet to the rest of us, could have nerved her to such an act.

My one hope, then, of understanding the matter lay with her. To seek her at once in the place where I had been told she awaited me seemed the only course to take. If any real gratitude underlay the look of trust which she had given me at the termination of our last interview, she would reward my confidence in her by unbosoming herself to me.

I was at the door of the boudoir immediately upon forming this resolution. Finding it ajar, I pushed it softly open, and as softly entered. To my astonishment, the place was very dark. Not only had the shades been drawn down, but the shutters had been closed, so that it was with difficulty I detected the slight, black-robed figure which lay, face down, among the cushions of a lounge. She had evidently not heard my entrance, for she did not move; and, struck by her pathetic attitude, I advanced in a whirl of feeling which made me forget all conventionalities and everything else, in fact, but that I loved her and had the utmost confidence in her power to make me happy. Laying my hand softly on her head, I tenderly whispered:

"Look up, dear. Whatever barrier may have intervened between us has fallen. Look up and hear how I love you."

She thrilled as a woman only thrills when her secret soul is moved, and, rising with a certain grand movement, turned her face upon me, glorious with a feeling that not even the dimness of the room could hide.

Why, then, did my brain whirl and my heart collapse?

It was Gilbertine and not Dorothy who stood before me.

IX

IN THE LITTLE BOUDOIR

Never had a suspicion crossed my mind of any such explanation of our secret troubles. I had seen as much of one cousin as the other in my visits to Mrs. Lansing's house, but Gilbertine being from the first day of our acquaintance engaged to my friend Sinclair, I naturally did not presume to study her face for any signs of interest in myself, even if my sudden and uncontrollable passion for Dorothy had left me the heart to do so. Yet now, in the light of her unmistakable smile, of her beaming eyes from which all troublous thoughts seemed to have fled for ever, a thousand recollections forced themselves upon my attention which not only made me bewail my own blindness, but which served to explain the peculiar attitude always maintained toward me by Dorothy, and many other things which a moment before had seemed fraught with impenetrable mystery.

All this in the twinkling of an eye. Meanwhile, misled by my words, Gilbertine drew back a step and with her face still bright with the radiance I have mentioned, murmured in low, but full-toned accents:

"Not just yet! it is too soon. Let me simply enjoy the fact that I am free and that the courage to win my release came from my own suddenly acquired trust in Mr. Sinclair's goodness. Last night—" and she shuddered—"I saw only another way—a way the horrors of which I hardly realized. But God saved me from so dreadful, yea, so unnecessary a crime, and this morning—"

It was cruel to let her go on, cruel to stand there and allow this ardent if mistaken nature to unfold itself so ingenuously, while I with ear half-turned toward the door, listened for the step of her whom I had never so much loved as at that moment—possibly because I had only just come to understand the cause of her seeming vacillations. My instincts were so imperative, my duty and the obligations of my position so unmistakable, that I made a move as she reached this point, which caused Gilbertine first to hesitate, then to stop. How should I fill up this gap of silence? How tell her of the great, the grievous mistake she had made? The task was one to try the courage of stouter souls than mine. But the thought of Dorothy nerved me; perhaps, also, my real friendship and commiseration for Sinclair.

"Gilbertine," I began, "I will make no pretense of misunderstanding you. The situation is too serious, the honor which you do me too great; only, I am not free to accept that honor. The words which I uttered were meant for your cousin Dorothy. I expected to find her in this room. I have long loved your cousin—in secrecy, I own, but honestly and with every hope of some day making her my wife. I—I—"

There was no need for me to finish. The warm hand turning to ice in my clasp, the wide-open, blind-struck eyes, the recoil, the maiden flush rising, deepening, covering chin and cheek and forehead, then fading out again till the whole face was white as marble and seemingly as cold—told me that the blow had gone home and that Gilbertine Murray, the unequalled beauty, the petted darling of a society who recognized every charm she possessed save her ardent nature and great heart, had reached the height of her many miseries and that it was I who had placed her there.

Overcome with pity, but conscious, also, of a profound respect, I endeavored to utter some futile words, which she at once put an end to by an appealing gesture.

"You can say nothing," she began. "I have made an awful mistake, the worst a woman can make, I think." Then, with long pauses, as though her tongue were clogged by shame—perhaps by some deeper if less apparent feeling—"You love Dorothy; does Dorothy love you?"

My answer was an honest one.

"I have dared to hope so, despite the little opportunity she has given me to express my feelings. She has always held me back, and that very decidedly, or my devotion would have been apparent to everybody."

"Oh, Dorothy!"

Regret, sorrow, infinite tenderness, all were audible in that cry. Indeed, it seemed as if for the moment her thoughts were more taken up with her cousin's unhappiness than with her own.

"How I must have made her suffer! I have been a curse to those who loved me. But I am humbled now, and very rightly."

I began to experience a certain awe of this great nature. There was grandeur even in her contrition and, as I took in the expression of her colorless features, sweet with almost an unearthly sweetness in spite of the anguish consuming her, I suddenly realized what Sinclair's love for her must be. I also as suddenly realized the depth and extent of his suffering. To call such a woman his, to lead her almost to the foot of the altar and then to see her turn aside and leave him! Surely his lot was an intolerable one, and, though the interference I had unconsciously made in his wishes had been involuntary, I felt like cursing myself for not having been more open in my attentions to the girl I really loved.

Gilbertine seemed to divine my thoughts, for, pausing at the door she had unconsciously approached, she stood with the knob in her hand, and, with averted brow, remarked gravely:

"I am going out of your life. Before I do so, however, I should like to say a few words in palliation of my conduct. I have never known a mother. I early fell under my aunt's charge, who, detesting children, sent me away to school, where I was well enough treated, but never loved. I was a plain child and felt my plainness. This gave an awkwardness to my actions, and as my aunt had caused it to be distinctly understood that her sole intention in sending me to the Academy was to have me educated for a teacher, my position awakened little interest, and few hearts, if any, warmed toward me. Meanwhile my breast was filled with but one thought, one absorbing wish. I longed to love passionately and be passionately loved in return. Had I found a mate—but I never did. I was not destined for any such happiness.

"Years passed. I was a woman, but neither my happiness nor my self-confidence had kept pace with my growth. Girls who once passed me with a bare nod now stopped to stare, sometimes to whisper comments behind my back. I did not understand this change, and withdrew more and more into myself and the fairy-land made for me by books. Romance was my life, and I had fallen into the dangerous habit of brooding over the pleasures and excitements which would have been mine had I been born beautiful and wealthy, when my aunt suddenly visited the school, saw me and at once took me away and placed me in the most fashionable school in New York City. From there I was launched, without any word of motherly counsel, into the gay society you know so well. Almost with my coming-out I found the world at my feet and, though my aunt showed me no love, she evinced a certain pride in my success and cast about to procure for me a great match. Mr. Sinclair was the victim. He visited me, took me to theaters and eventually proposed. My aunt was in ecstasies. I, who felt helpless before her will, was glad that the husband she had chosen for me was, at least, a gentleman, and, to all appearances, respectable in his living and nice in his tastes. But he was not the man I had dwelt on in my dreams, and while I accepted him—(it was not possible to do anything else, with my aunt controlling every action, if not every thought)—I cared so little for Mr. Sinclair himself that I forgot to ask if his many attentions were the result of any real feeling on his part or only such as he considered due to the woman he expected to make his wife. You see what girls are. How I despise myself now for this miserable frivolity!

"All this time I knew that I was not my aunt's only niece; that Dorothy Camerden, of whom I knew little but her name, was as closely related to her as I was. For, true to her heartless code, my aunt had placed us in separate schools and we had never met. When she found that I was to leave her and that soon there would be nobody to see that her dresses were bought with discretion, and her person attended to with something like care, she sent for Dorothy. I shall never forget my first impression of her. I had been told that I need not expect much in the way of beauty and style, but from my first glimpse of her dear face, I saw that my soul's friend had come and that, marriage or no marriage, I need never be solitary again.

"I do not think I made as favorable an impression on my cousin as she did on me. Dorothy was new to elaborate dressing and to all the follies of fashionable life, and her look had more of awe than expectation in it. But I gave her a hearty kiss and in a week she was as brilliantly equipped as myself.

"I loved her, but, from blindness of eye or an overwhelming egotism which God has certainly punished, I did not consider her beautiful. This I must acknowledge to you, if only to complete my humiliation. I never imagined for a moment, even after I became the daily witness of your many attentions to her, that it was on her account you visited the house so often. I had been so petted and spoiled since entering society that I thought you were kind to her simply because honor forbade you to be too kind to me; and seeing in you a man different from the others—one—who—who pleased me as the heroes of my old romances had pleased me, I gave you all my heart and, what was worse, *confided my folly to Dorothy*.

"You will have many a talk with her in the future, and some day she may succeed in proving to you that it was vanity and not badness of heart which led me to misunderstand your feelings. Having repressed my own impulses so long, I saw in your reticence the evidences of a like struggle; and when, immediately upon my break with Mr. Sinclair, you entered here and said the words you did—Well, we have finished with this subject for ever.

"The explanations which I gave below, of the part I played in my aunt's death were true. I only omitted one detail, which you may consider a very important one. The fact which paralyzed my hand and voice when I saw her lift the drop of death to her lips was this: I had meant to die by this drop myself, in Dorothy's room, and with Dorothy's arms about me. This was my secret—a secret which no one can blame me for keeping as long as I could, and one which I should hardly have the courage to disclose to you now if I had not already parted with it to the coroner, who would not credit my story till I had told him the whole truth."

"Gilbertine," I prayed, for I saw her fingers closing upon the knob she had held lightly till now, "do not go till I have said this. A young girl does not always know the demands of her own nature. The heart you have ignored is one in a thousand. Do not let it slip from you. God never gives a woman such a love twice."

"I know it," she murmured, and turned the knob.

I thought she was gone, and let the sigh which had been laboring at my breast have vent, when suddenly I caught one last word whispered from the threshold:

"Throw back the shutters and let in the light. Dorothy is coming. I am going now to call her."

An hour had passed, the hour of hours for me, for in it the sun of my happiness rose full-orbed and Dorothy and I came to understand each other. We were sitting hand in hand in this blessed little boudoir, when suddenly she turned her sweet face toward me and gently remarked:

"This seems like selfishness on our part; but Gilbertine insisted. Do you know what she is doing now? Helping old Mrs. Cummings and holding Mrs. Barnstable's baby while her maid packs. She will work like that all day, and with a smile, too. Oh, it is a rich nature, an ideal nature! I think we can trust her now."

I did not like to discuss Gilbertine even with Dorothy, so I said nothing. But she was too full of her theme to stop. I think she wished to unburden her mind once and for ever of all that had disturbed it.

"Our aunt's death," she continued, "will be a sort of emancipation for her. I don't think you, or any one out of our immediate household, can realize the control which Aunt Hannah exerted over every one who came within her daily influence. It would have been the same had she occupied a dependent position instead of being the wealthy autocrat she was. In her cold nature dwelt an imperiousness which no one could withstand. You know how her friends, some of them as rich and influential as herself, bowed to her will and submitted to her interference. What, then, could you expect from two poor girls entirely dependent upon her for everything they enjoyed? Gilbertine, with all her spirit, could not face Aunt Hannah's frown, while I studied to have no wishes. Had this been otherwise, had we found a friend instead of a tyrant in the woman who took us into her home, Gilbertine might have gained more control over her feelings. It was the necessity she felt of smothering her natural impulses, and of maintaining in the house and before the world an appearance of satisfaction in her position as bride-elect, which caused her to fall into such extremes of despondency and deep despair. Her self-respect was shocked. She felt that she was living a lie and hated herself in consequence.

"You may think I did wrong not to tell her of your affection for myself, especially, after what you whispered into my ear that night at the theater. I did do wrong; I see it now. She was really a stronger woman than I thought and we might all have been saved the horrors which have befallen us had I acted with more firmness at that time. But I was weak and frightened. I held you back and let her go on deceiving herself, which meant deceiving Mr. Sinclair, too. I thought, when she found herself really married and settled in her own home, she would find it easier to forget, and that soon, perhaps very soon, all this would seem like a troubled dream to her. And there was reason for this hope on my part. She showed a woman's natural interest in her outfit and the plans for her new house, but when she heard you were to be Mr. Sinclair's best man, every feminine instinct within her rebelled and it was with difficulty she could prevent herself from breaking out into a loud No! in face of aunt and lover. From this moment on her state of mind grew desperate. In the parlor, at the theater, she was the brilliant girl whom all admired and many envied; but in my little room at night she would bury her face in my lap and talk of death, till I moved in a constant atmosphere of dread. Yet, because she looked gay and laughed, I turned a like face to the world and laughed also. We felt it was expected of us, and the very nervous tension we were under made these ebullitions easy. But I did not laugh so much after coming here. One night I found her out of her bed long after every one else had retired for the night. Next morning Mr. Beaton told a dream—I hope it was a dream—but it frightened me. Then came that moment when Mr. Sinclair displayed the amethyst box and explained with such a nonchalant air how a drop from the little flask inside would kill a person. A toy, but so deadly! I felt the thrill which shot like lightning through her, and made up my mind she should never have the opportunity of touching that box. And that is why I stole into the library at the first moment I had to myself and took down the little box and hid it in my hair. I never thought to look inside; I did not pause to think that it was the flask and not the box she wanted, and consequently felt convinced of her safety so long as I kept the latter successfully concealed in my hair. You know the rest."

Yes, I knew it. How she opened the box in her room and found it empty. How she flew to Gilbertine's room, and, finding the door unlocked, looked in, and saw Miss Lane lying there asleep but no Gilbertine. How her alarm grew at this and how, forgetting that her cousin often stole to her room by means of the connecting balcony, she had wandered over the house in the hope of coming upon Gilbertine in one of the down-stairs rooms. How her mind misgave her before she had entered the great hall, and how she turned back only to hear that awful scream go up as she was setting foot upon the spiral stair. I had heard it all before and could imagine her terror and dismay; and why she found it impossible to proceed any further, but clung to the stair-rail, half-alive and half-dead, till she was found there by those seeking her and taken up to her aunt's room. But she never told me, and I do not yet know, what her thoughts or feelings were when, instead of seeing her cousin outstretched in death on the bed they led her to, she beheld the lifeless figure of her aunt. The reserve she maintained on this point has been always respected by me. Let it continue to be so.

When therefore she said, "You know the rest," I took her in my arms and gave her my first kiss. Then I softly released her, and by tacit consent we each went our way for that day.

Mine took me into the hall below, which was all alive with the hum of departing guests. Beaton was among them, and as he stepped out on the porch I gave him a parting handclasp and quietly whispered:

"When all dark things are made light, you will find that there was both more and less to your dream than you were inclined to make out."

He bowed, and that was the last word which ever passed between us on this topic.

But what chiefly impressed me in connection with this afternoon's events was the short talk I had with Sinclair. I feared I forced this talk, but I could not let the dreary day settle into still drearier night without making clear to him a point which, in the new position he held toward Gilbertine if not toward myself, might seem to be involved in some doubt. When, therefore, I had the opportunity to accost him I did so, and, without noting the formal bow with which he strove to hold back all confidential communication, I said:

"It is not a very propitious time for me to intrude my personal affairs upon you, but I feel as if I should like you to know that the clouds have been cleared away between Dorothy and myself, and that some day we expect to marry."

He gave me the earnest look of a man who has recovered his one friend. Then he grasped my hand warmly, saying with something like his old fervor:

"You deserve all the happiness that awaits you. Mine is gone; but if I can regain it, I will; trust me for that, Worthington."

The coroner, who had seen much of life and human nature, managed with much discretion the inquest he felt bound to hold. Mrs. Lansing was found to have come to her death by a meddlesome interference with one of her niece's wedding trinkets; and, as every one acquainted with Mrs. Lansing knew her to be quite capable of such an act of malicious folly, the verdict was duly accepted and the real heart of this tragedy closed for ever from every human eye.

As we were leaving Newport Sinclair stepped up to me.

"I have reason to know," said he, "that Mrs. Lansing's bequests will be a surprise, not only to her nieces, but to the world at large. Let me advise you to announce your engagement before reaching New York."

I followed his advice and in a few days understood why it had been given. All the vast property owned by this woman had been left to Dorothy. Gilbertine had been cut off without a cent.

We never knew Mrs. Lansing's reason for this act. Gilbertine had always been considered her favorite, and, had the will been a late one, it would have been generally thought that she had left her thus unprovided for solely in consideration of the great match which she expected her to make. But the will was dated back several years,—long before Gilbertine had met Mr. Sinclair, long before either niece had come to live with Mrs. Lansing in New York. Had it always been the latter's wish, then, to enrich the one and slight the other? It would seem so, but why should the slighted one be Gilbertine?

The only explanation I ever heard given was the partiality which Mrs. Lansing felt for Dorothy's mother, or, rather, her lack of affection for Gilbertine's. God knows if it is the true one, but whether so or not, the discrimination she showed in her will put poor Gilbertine in a very unfortunate position. At least, it would have done so, if Sinclair, with an adroitness worthy of his love, had not proved to her that a break at this time in their supposed relations would reflect most seriously upon his disinterestedness and thus secured for himself opportunities for urging his suit which ended, as such opportunities often do, in a renewal of their engagement. But this time mutual love was its basis. This was evident to any one who saw them together. But how the magic was wrought, how this hard-to-be-won heart learned at last its true allegiance, I did not know till later, and then it was told me by Gilbertine herself.

I had been married for some months and she for some weeks, when one evening chance threw us together. Instantly, and as if she had waited for this hour, she turned upon me with the beautiful smile which has been hers ever since her new happiness came to her, and said:

"You once gave me some very good advice, Mr. Worthington, but it was not that which led me to realize Mr. Sinclair's affection. It was a short conversation which passed between us on the day my aunt's will was read. Do you remember my turning to speak to him the moment after that word *all* fell from the lawyer's lips?"

"Yes, Mrs. Sinclair." Alas! did I not! It was one of the most poignant memories of my life. The look she gave him, and the look he gave her! Indeed, I did remember.

"It was to ask him one question,—a question to which misfortune only could have given so much weight. Had my aunt taken him into her confidence? Had he known that I had no place in her will? His answer was very simple; a single word,—'always.' But after that, do I need to say why I am a wife? why I am *his* wife?"

THE HOUSE IN THE MIST

I

AN OPEN DOOR

It was a night to drive any man indoors. Not only was the darkness impenetrable, but the raw mist enveloping hill and valley made the open road anything but desirable to a belated wayfarer like myself.

Being young, untrammeled, and naturally indifferent to danger, I was not averse to adventure; and having my fortune to make, was always on the lookout for El Dorado, which, to ardent souls, lies ever beyond the next turning. Consequently, when I saw a light shimmering through the mist at my right, I resolved to make for it and the shelter it so opportunely offered.

But I did not realize then, as I do now, that shelter does not necessarily imply refuge, or I might not have undertaken this adventure with so light a heart. Yet, who knows? The impulses of an unfettered spirit lean toward daring, and youth, as I have said, seeks the strange, the unknown and, sometimes, the terrible.

My path toward this light was by no means an easy one. After confused wanderings through tangled hedges, and a struggle with obstacles of whose nature I received the most curious impression in the surrounding murk, I arrived in front of a long, low building which, to my astonishment, I found standing with doors and windows open to the pervading mist, save for one square casement through which the light shone from a row of candles placed on a long mahogany table.

The quiet and seeming emptiness of this odd and picturesque building made me pause. I am not much affected by visible danger, but this silent room, with its air of sinister expectancy, struck me most unpleasantly, and I was about to reconsider my first impulse and withdraw again to the road, when a second look, thrown back upon the comfortable interior I was leaving, convinced me of my folly and sent me straight toward the door which stood so invitingly open.

But half-way up the path, my progress was again stayed by the sight of a man issuing from the house I had so rashly looked upon as devoid of all human presence. He seemed in haste and, at the moment my eye first fell on him, was engaged in replacing his watch in his pocket.

But he did not shut the door behind him, which I thought odd, especially as his final glance had been a backward one, and seemed to take in all the appointments of the place he was so hurriedly leaving.

As we met, he raised his hat. This likewise struck me as peculiar, for the deference he displayed was more marked than that usually bestowed on strangers, while his lack of surprise at an encounter more or less startling in such a mist was calculated to puzzle an ordinary man like myself. Indeed, he was so little impressed by my presence there that he was for passing me without a word or any other hint of good fellowship, save the bow of which I have spoken. But this did not suit me. I was hungry, cold, and eager for creature comforts, and the house before me gave forth not only heat, but a savory odor which in itself was an invitation hard to ignore. I therefore accosted the man.

"Will bed and supper be provided me here?" I asked. "I am tired out with a long tramp over the hills, and hungry enough to pay anything in reason—"

I stopped, for the man had disappeared. He had not paused at my appeal and the mist had swallowed him. But at the break in my sentence, his voice came back in good-natured tones and I heard:

"Supper will be ready at nine, and there are beds for all. Enter, sir; you are the first to arrive, but the others can not be far behind."

A queer greeting, certainly. But when I strove to question him as to its meaning, his voice returned to me from such a distance that I doubted if my words had reached him with any more distinctness than his answer reached me.

"Well!" thought I, "it isn't as if a lodging had been denied me. He invited me to enter, and enter I will."

The house, to which I now naturally directed a glance of much more careful scrutiny than before, was no ordinary farm-building, but a rambling old mansion, made conspicuously larger here and there by jutting porches and more than one convenient lean-to. Though furnished, warmed and lighted with candles, as I have previously described, it had about it an air of disuse which made me feel myself an intruder, in spite of the welcome I had received. But I was not in a position to stand upon ceremony, and ere long I found myself inside the great room and before the blazing logs whose glow had lighted up the doorway and added its own attraction to the other allurements of the inviting place.

Though the open door made a draft which was anything but pleasant, I did not feel like closing it, and was astonished to observe the effect of the mist through the square thus left open to the night. It was not an agreeable one, and, instinctively turning my back upon that quarter of the room, I let my eyes roam over the wainscoted walls and the odd pieces of furniture which gave such an air of old-fashioned richness to the place. As nothing of the kind had ever fallen under my eyes before, I should have thoroughly enjoyed this opportunity of gratifying my taste for the curious and the beautiful, if the quaint old chairs I saw standing about me on every side had not all been empty. But the solitude of the place, so much more oppressive than the solitude of the road I had left, struck cold to my heart, and I missed the cheer rightfully belonging to such attractive surroundings. Suddenly I bethought me of the many other apartments likely to be found in so spacious a dwelling, and, going to the nearest door, I opened it and called out for the master of the house. But only an echo came back, and, returning to the fire, I sat down before the cheering blaze, in quiet acceptance of a situation too lonely for comfort, yet not without a certain piquant interest for a man of free mind and adventurous disposition like myself.

After all, if supper was to be served at nine, someone must be expected to eat it: I should surely not be left much longer without companions.

Meanwhile ample amusement awaited me in the contemplation of a picture which, next to the large fireplace, was the most prominent object in the room. This picture was a portrait, and a remarkable one. The countenance it portrayed was both characteristic and forcible, and so interested me that in studying it I quite forgot both hunger and weariness. Indeed its effect upon me was such that, after gazing at it uninterruptedly for a few minutes, I discovered that its various features—the narrow eyes in which a hint of craft gave a strange gleam to their native intelligence; the steadfast chin, strong as the rock of the hills I had wearily tramped all day; the cunning wrinkles which yet did not interfere with a latent great-heartedness that made the face as attractive as it was puzzling—had so established themselves in my mind that I continued to see them before me whichever way I turned, and found it impossible to shake off their influence even after I had resolutely set my mind in another direction by endeavoring to recall what I knew of the town into which I had strayed.

I had come from Scranton and was now, according to my best judgment, in one of those rural districts of western Pennsylvania which breed such strange and sturdy characters. But of this special neighborhood, its inhabitants and its industries, I knew nothing nor was likely to, so long as I remained in the solitude I have endeavored to describe.

But these impressions and these thoughts—if thoughts they were—presently received a check. A loud "Halloo" rose from somewhere in the mist, followed by a string of muttered imprecations, which convinced me that the person now attempting to approach the house was encountering some of the many difficulties which had beset me in the same undertaking a few minutes before.

I therefore raised my voice and shouted out, "Here! this way!" after which I sat still and awaited developments.

There was a huge clock in one of the corners, whose loud tick filled up every interval of silence. By this clock it was just ten minutes to eight when two gentlemen (I should say men, and coarse men at that) crossed the open threshold and entered the house.

Their appearance was more or less note-worthy—unpleasantly so, I am obliged to add. One was red-faced and obese, the other was tall, thin and wiry and showed as many seams in his face as a blighted apple. Neither of the two had anything to recommend him either in appearance or address, save a certain veneer of polite assumption as transparent as it was offensive. As I listened to the forced sallies of the one and the hollow laugh of the other, I was glad that I was large of frame and strong of arm and used to all kinds of men and—brutes.

As these two new-comers seemed no more astonished at my presence than the man I had met at the gate, I checked the question which instinctively rose to my lips and with a simple bow,—responded to by a more or less familiar nod from either,—accepted the situation with all the *sang-froid* the occasion seemed to demand. Perhaps this was wise, perhaps it was not; there was little opportunity to judge, for the start they both gave as they encountered the eyes of the picture before mentioned drew my attention to a consideration of the different ways in which men, however similar in other respects, express sudden and unlooked-for emotion. The big man simply allowed his astonishment, dread, or whatever the feeling was which moved him, to ooze forth in a cold and deathly perspiration which robbed his cheeks of color and cast a bluish shadow over his narrow and retreating temples; while the thin and waspish man, caught in the same trap (for trap I saw it was), shouted aloud in his ill-timed mirth, the false and cruel character of which would have made me shudder, if all expression of feeling on my part had not been held in check by the interest I immediately experienced in the display of open bravado with which, in another moment, these two tried to carry off their mutual embarrassment.

"Good likeness, eh?" laughed the seamy-faced man. "Quite an idea, that! Makes him one of us again! Well, he's welcome—in oils. Can't say much to us from canvas, eh?" And the rafters above him vibrated, as his violent efforts at joviality went up in loud and louder assertion from his thin throat.

A nudge from the other's elbow stopped him and I saw them both cast half-lowering, half-inquisitive glances in my direction.

"One of the Witherspoon boys?" queried one.

"Perhaps," snarled the other. "I never saw but one of them. There are five, aren't there? Eustace believed in marrying off his gals young."

"Damn him, yes. And he'd have married them off younger if he had known how numbers were going to count some day among the Westonhaughs." And he laughed again in a way I should certainly have felt it my business to resent, if my indignation as well as the ill-timed allusions which had called it forth had not been put to an end by a fresh arrival through the veiling mist which hung like a shroud at the doorway.

This time it was for me to experience a shock of something like fear. Yet the personage who called up this unlooked-for sensation in my naturally hardy nature was old and, to all appearance, harmless from disability, if not from good will. His form was bent over upon itself like a bow; and only from the glances he shot from his upturned eyes was the fact made evident that a redoubtable nature, full of force and malignity, had just brought its quota of evil into a room already overflowing with dangerous and menacing passions.

As this old wretch, either from the feebleness of age or from the infirmity I have mentioned, had great difficulty in walking, he had brought with him a small boy, whose business it was to direct his tottering steps as best he could.

But once settled in his chair, he drove away this boy with his pointed oak stick, and with some harsh words about caring for the horse and being on time in the morning, he sent him out into the mist. As this little shivering and pathetic figure vanished, the old man drew, with gasp and haw, a number of deep breaths which shook his bent back and did their share, no doubt, in restoring his own disturbed circulation. Then, with a sinister twist which brought his pointed chin and twinkling eyes again into view, he remarked:

"Haven't ye a word for kinsman Luke, you two? It isn't often I get out among ye. Shakee, nephew! Shakee, Hector! And now who's the boy in the window? My eyes aren't what they used to be, but he don't seem to favor the Westonhaughs over-much. One of Salmon's four grandchildren, think 'e? Or a shoot from Eustace's gnarled old trunk? His gals all married Americans, and one of them, I've been told, was a yellow-haired giant like this fellow."

As this description pointed directly toward me, I was about to venture a response on my own account, when my attention, as well as theirs, was freshly attracted by a loud "Whoa!" at the gate, followed by the hasty but assured entrance of a dapper, wizen, but perfectly preserved little old gentleman with a bag in his hand. Looking askance with eyes that were like two beads, first at the two men who were now elbowing each other for the best place before the fire, and then at the revolting figure in the chair, he bestowed his greeting, which consisted of an elaborate bow, not on them, but upon the picture hanging so conspicuously on the open wall before him; and then, taking me within the scope of his quick, circling glance, cried out with an assumption of great cordiality:

"Good evening, gentlemen; good evening one, good evening all. Nothing like being on the tick. I'm sorry the night has turned out so badly. Some may find it too thick for travel. That would be bad, eh? very bad—for *them*."

As none of the men he openly addressed saw fit to answer, save by the hitch of a shoulder or a leer quickly suppressed, I kept silent also. But this reticence, marked as it was, did not seem to offend the new-comer. Shaking the wet from the umbrella he held, he stood the dripping article up in a corner and then came and placed his feet on the fender. To do this he had to crowd between the two men already occupying the best part of the hearth. But he showed no concern at incommoding them, and bore their cross looks and threatening gestures with professional equanimity.

"You know me?" he now unexpectedly snapped, bestowing another look over his shoulder at that oppressive figure in the chair. (Did I say that I had risen when the latter sat?) "I'm no Westonhaugh, I; nor yet a Witherspoon nor a Clapsaddle. I'm only Smead, the lawyer. Mr. Anthony Westonhaugh's lawyer," he repeated, with another glance of recognition in the direction of the picture. "I drew up his last will and testament, and, until all of his wishes have been duly carried out, am entitled by the terms of that will to be regarded both legally and socially as his representative. This you all know, but it is my way to make everything clear as I proceed. A lawyer's trick, no doubt. I do not pretend to be entirely exempt from such."

A grumble from the large man, who seemed to have been disturbed in some absorbing calculation he was carrying on, mingled with a few muttered words of forced acknowledgment from the restless old sinner in the chair, made it unnecessary for me to reply, even if the last comer had given me the opportunity.

"It's getting late!" he cried, with an easy garrulity rather amusing, under the circumstances. "Two more trains came in as I left the depot. If old Phil was on hand with his wagon, several more members of this interesting family may be here before the clock strikes; if not, the assemblage is like to be small. Too small," I heard him grumble a minute after, under his breath.

"I wish it were a matter of one," spoke up the big man, striking his breast in a way to make it perfectly apparent whom he meant by that word *one*. And having (if I may judge by the mingled laugh and growl of his companions) thus shown his hand both figuratively and literally, he relapsed into the calculation which seemed to absorb all of his unoccupied moments.

"Generous, very!" commented the lawyer in a murmur which was more than audible. "Pity that sentiments of such broad benevolence should go unrewarded."

This, because at that very instant wheels were heard in front, also a jangle of voices, in some controversy about fares, which promised anything but a pleasing addition to the already none too desirable company.

"I suppose that's sister Janet," snarled out the one addressed as Hector. There was no love in his voice, despite the relationship hinted at, and I awaited the entrance of this woman with some curiosity.

But her appearance, heralded by many a puff and pant which the damp air exaggerated in a prodigious way, did not seem to warrant the interest I had shown in it. As she stepped into the room, I saw only a big frowsy woman, who had attempted to make a show with a new silk dress and a hat in the latest fashion, but who had lamentably failed, owing to the slouchiness of her figure and some misadventure by which her hat had been set awry on her head and her usual complacency destroyed. Later, I noted that her down-looking eyes had a false twinkle in them, and that, commonplace as she looked, she was one to steer clear of in times of necessity and distress.

She, too, evidently expected to find the door open and people assembled, but she had not anticipated being confronted by the portrait on the wall, and cringed in an unpleasant way as she stumbled by it into one of the ill-lighted corners.

The old man, who had doubtless caught the rustle of her dress as she passed him, emitted one short sentence.

"Almost late," said he.

Her answer was a sputter of words.

"It's the fault of that driver," she complained. "If he had taken one drop more at the half-way house, I might really not have got here at all. That would not have inconvenienced *you*. But oh! what a grudge I would have owed that skinflint brother of ours" —here she shook her fist at the picture—"for making our good luck depend upon our arrival within two short strokes of the clock!"

"There are several to come yet," blandly observed the lawyer. But before the words were well out of his mouth, we all became aware of a new presence—a woman, whose somber grace and quiet bearing gave distinction to her unobtrusive entrance, and caused a feeling of something like awe to follow the first sight of her cold features and deep, heavily-fringed eyes. But this soon passed in the more human sentiment awakened by the soft pleading which infused her gaze with a touching femininity. She wore a long loose garment which fell without a fold from chin to foot, and in her arms she seemed to carry something.

Never before had I seen so beautiful a woman. As I was contemplating her, with respect but yet with a masculine intentness I could not quite suppress, two or three other persons came in. And now I began to notice that the eyes of all these people turned mainly one way, and that was toward the clock. Another small circumstance likewise drew my attention. Whenever any one entered,—and there were one or two additional arrivals during the five minutes preceding the striking of the hour,—a frown settled for an instant on every brow, giving to each and all a similar look, for the interpretation of which I lacked the key. Yet not on every brow either. There was one which remained undisturbed and showed only a grand patience.

As the hands of the big clock neared the point of eight, a furtive smile appeared on more than one face; and when the hour rang out, a sigh of satisfaction swept through the room, to which the little old lawyer responded with a worldly-wise grunt, as he moved from his place and proceeded to the door.

This he had scarcely shut when a chorus of voices rose from without. Three or four lingerers had pushed their way as far as the gate, only to see the door of the house shut in their faces.

"Too late!" growled old man Luke from between the locks of his long beard.

"Too late!" shrieked the woman who had come so near being late herself.

"Too late!" smoothly acquiesced the lawyer, locking and bolting the door with a deft and assured hand.

But the four or five persons who thus found themselves barred out did not accept without a struggle the decision of the more fortunate ones assembled within. More than one hand began pounding on the door, and we could hear cries of, "The train was behind time!" "Your clock is fast!" "You are cheating us; you want it all for yourselves!" "We will have the law on you!" and other bitter adjurations unintelligible to me from my ignorance of the circumstances which called them forth.

But the wary old lawyer simply shook his head and answered nothing; whereat a murmur of gratification rose from within, and a howl of almost frenzied dismay from without, which latter presently received point from a startling vision which now appeared at the casement where the lights burned. A man's face looked in, and behind it, that of a woman, so wild and maddened by some sort of heart-break that I found my sympathies aroused in spite of the glare of evil passions which made both of these countenances something less than human.

But the lawyer met the stare of these four eyes with a quiet chuckle, which found its echo in the ill-advised mirth of those about him; and moving over to the window where they still peered in, he drew together the two heavy shutters which hitherto had stood back against the wall, and, fastening them with a bar, shut out the sight of this despair, if he could not shut out the protests which ever and anon were shouted through the keyhole.

Meanwhile, one form had sat through this whole incident without a gesture; and on the quiet brow, from which I could not keep my eyes, no shadows appeared save the perpetual one of native melancholy, which was at once the source of its attraction and the secret of its power.

Into what sort of gathering had I stumbled? And why did I prefer to await developments rather than ask the simplest question of any one about me?

Meantime the lawyer had proceeded to make certain preparations. With the help of one or two willing hands, he had drawn the great table into the middle of the room and, having seen the candles restored to their places, began to open his small bag and take from it a roll of paper and several flat documents. Laying the latter in the center of the table and slowly unrolling the former, he consulted, with his foxy eyes, the faces surrounding him, and smiled with secret malevolence, as he noted that every chair and every form were turned away from the picture before which he had bent with such obvious courtesy, on entering. I alone stood erect, and this possibly was why a gleam of curiosity was noticeable in his glance, as he ended his scrutiny of my countenance and bent his gaze again upon the paper he held.

"Heavens!" thought I. "What shall I answer this man if he asks me why I continued to remain in a spot where I have so little business." The impulse came to go. But such was the effect of this strange convocation of persons, at night and in a mist which was itself a nightmare, that I failed to take action and remained riveted to my place, while Mr. Smead consulted his roll and finally asked in a business-like tone, quite unlike his previous sarcastic speech, the names of those whom he had the pleasure of seeing before him.

The old man in the chair spoke up first.

"Luke Westonhaugh," he announced.

"Very good!" responded the lawyer.

"Hector Westonhaugh," came from the thin man.

A nod and a look toward the next.

"John Westonhaugh."

"Nephew?" asked the lawyer.

"Yes."

"Go on, and be quick; supper will be ready at nine."

"Eunice Westonhaugh," spoke up a soft voice.

I felt my heart bound as if some inner echo responded to that name.

"Daughter of whom?"

"Hudson Westonhaugh," she gently faltered. "My father is dead—died last night;—I am his only heir."

A grumble of dissatisfaction and a glint of unrelieved hate came from the doubled-up figure, whose malevolence had so revolted me.

But the lawyer was not to be shaken.

"Very good! It is fortunate you trusted your feet rather than the train. And now you! What is your name?"

He was looking, not at me as I had at first feared, but at the man next to me, a slim but slippery youth, whose small red eyes made me shudder.

"William Witherspoon."

"Barbara's son?"

"Yes."

"Where are your brothers?"

"One of them, I think, is outside"—here he laughed;—"the other is—*sick*."

The way he uttered this word made me set him down as one to be especially wary of when he smiled. But then I had already passed judgment on him at my first view.

"And you, madam?"—this to the large, dowdy woman with the uncertain eye, a contrast to the young and melancholy Eunice.

"Janet Clapsaddle," she replied, waddling hungrily forward and getting unpleasantly near the speaker, for he moved off as she approached, and took his stand in the clear place at the head of the table.

"Very good, Mistress Clapsaddle. You were a Westonhaugh, I believe?"

"You *believe*, sneak-faced hypocrite that you are!" she blurted out. "I don't understand your lawyer ways. I like plain speaking myself. Don't you know me, and Luke and Hector, and—and most of us indeed, except that puny, white-faced girl yonder, whom, having been brought up on the other side of the Ridge, we have none of us seen since she was a screaming baby in Hildegarde's arms. And the young gentleman over there,"—here she indicated me—"who shows so little likeness to the rest of the family. He will have to make it pretty plain who his father was before we shall feel like acknowledging him, either as the son of one of Eustace's girls, or a chip from brother Salmon's hard old block."

As this caused all eyes to turn upon me, even *hers*, I smiled as I stepped forward. The lawyer did not return that smile.

"What is your name?" he asked shortly and sharply, as if he distrusted me.

"Hugh Austin," was my quiet reply.

"There is no such name on the list," snapped old Smead, with an authoritative gesture toward those who seemed anxious to enter a protest.

"Probably not," I returned, "for I am neither a Witherspoon, a Westonhaugh nor a Clapsaddle. I am merely a chance wayfarer passing through the town on my way west. I thought this house was a tavern, or at least a place I could lodge in. The man I met in the doorway told me as much, and so I am here. If my company is not agreeable, or if you wish this room to yourselves, let me go into the kitchen.

I promise not to meddle with the supper, hungry as I am. Or perhaps you wish me to join the crowd outside; it seems to be increasing."

"No, no," came from all parts of the room. "Don't let the door be opened. Nothing could keep Lemuel and his crowd out if they once got foot over the threshold."

The lawyer rubbed his chin. He seemed to be in some sort of quandary. First he scrutinized me from under his shaggy brows with a sharp gleam of suspicion; then his features softened and, with a side glance at the young woman who called herself Eunice, (perhaps, because she was worth looking at, perhaps because she had partly risen at my words), he slipped toward a door I had before observed in the wainscoting on the left of the mantelpiece, and softly opened it upon what looked like a narrow staircase.

"We can not let you go out," said he; "and we can not let you have a finger in our viands before the hour comes for serving them; so if you will be so good as to follow this staircase to the top, you will find it ends in a room comfortable enough for the wayfarer you call yourself. In that room you can rest till the way is clear for you to continue your travels. Better, we can not do for you. This house is not a tavern, but the somewhat valuable property of—" He turned with a bow and smile, as every one there drew a deep breath; but no one ventured to end that sentence.

I would have given all my future prospects (which, by the way, were not very great) to remain in that room. The oddity of the situation; the mystery of the occurrence; the suspense I saw in every face; the eagerness of the cries I heard redoubled from time to time outside; the malevolence but poorly disguised in the old lawyer's countenance; and, above all, the presence of that noble-looking woman, which was the one off-set to the general tone of villainy with which the room was charged, filled me with curiosity, if I might call it by no other name, that made my acquiescence in the demand thus made upon me positively heroic. But there seemed no other course for me to follow, and with a last lingering glance at the genial fire and a quick look about me, which happily encountered hers, I stooped my head to suit the low and narrow doorway opened for my accommodation, and instantly found myself in darkness. The door had been immediately closed by the lawyer's impatient hand.

II

WITH MY EAR TO THE WAINSCOTING

No move more unwise could have been made by the old lawyer,—that is, if his intention had been to rid himself of an unwelcome witness. For, finding myself thrust thus suddenly from the scene, I naturally stood still instead of mounting the stairs, and, by standing still, discovered that though shut from sight I was not from sound. Distinctly through the panel of the door, which was much thinner, no doubt, than the old fox imagined, I heard one of the men present shout out:

"Well, that makes the number less by *one!*"

The murmur which followed this remark came plainly to my ears, and, greatly rejoicing over what I considered my good luck, I settled myself on the lowest step of the stairs in the hope of catching some word which would reveal to me the mystery of this scene.

It was not long in coming. Old Smead had now his audience before him in good shape, and his next words were of a character to make evident the purpose of this meeting.

"Heirs of Anthony Westonhaugh, deceased," he began in a sing-song voice strangely unmusical, "I congratulate you upon your good fortune at being at this especial moment on the inner rather than outer side of your amiable relative's front door. His will, which you have assembled to hear read, is well known to you. By it his whole property—(not so large as some of you might wish, but yet a goodly property for farmers like yourselves)—is to be divided this night, share and share alike, among such of his relatives as have found it convenient to be present here between the strokes of half-past seven and eight. If some of our friends have failed us through sloth, sickness or the misfortune of mistaking the road, they have our sympathy, but they can not have *his dollars.*"

"Can not have his dollars!" echoed a rasping voice which, from its smothered sound, probably came from the bearded lips of the old reprobate in the chair.

The lawyer waited for one or two other repetitions of this phrase (a phrase which, for some unimaginable reason, seemed to give him an odd sort of pleasure), then he went on with greater distinctness and a certain sly emphasis, chilling in effect but very professional:

"Ladies and gentlemen: Shall I read this will?"

"No, no! The division! the division! Tell us what we are to have!" rose in a shout about him.

There was a pause. I could imagine the sharp eyes of the lawyer traveling from face to face as each thus gave voice to his cupidity, and the thin curl of his lips as he remarked in a slow tantalizing way:

"There was more in the old man's clutches than you think."

A gasp of greed shook the partition against which my ear was pressed. Some one must have drawn up against the wainscoting since my departure from the room. I found myself wondering which of them it was. Meantime old Smead was having his say, with the smoothness of a man who perfectly understands what is required of him.

"Mr. Westonhaugh would not have put you to so much trouble or had you wait so long if he had not expected to reward you amply. There are shares in this bag which are worth thousands instead of hundreds. Now, now! stop that! hands off! hands off! there are calculations to make first. How many of you are there? Count up, some of you."

"Nine!" called out a voice with such rapacious eagerness that the word was almost unintelligible.

"Nine." How slowly the old knave spoke! What pleasure he seemed to take in the suspense he purposely made as exasperating as possible!

"Well, if each one gets his share, he may count himself richer by two hundred thousand dollars than when he came in here to-night."

Two hundred thousand dollars! They had expected no more than thirty. Surprise made them speechless, — that is, for a moment; then a pandemonium of hurrahs, shrieks and loud-voiced enthusiasm made the room ring, till wonder seized them again, and a sudden silence fell, through which I caught a far-off wail of grief from the disappointed ones without, which, heard in the dark and narrow place in which I was confined, had a peculiarly weird and desolate effect.

Perhaps it likewise was heard by some of the fortunate ones within! Perhaps one head, to mark which, in this moment of universal elation, I would have given a year from my life, turned toward the dark without, in recognition of the despair thus piteously voiced; but if so, no token of the same came to me, and I could but hope that she had shown, by some such movement, the natural sympathy of her sex.

Meanwhile the lawyer was addressing the company in his smoothest and most sarcastic tones.

"Mr. Westonhaugh was a wise man, a very wise man," he droned. "He foresaw what your pleasure would be, and left a letter for you. But before I read it, before I invite you to the board he ordered to be spread for you in honor of this happy occasion, there is one appeal he bade me make to those I should find assembled here. As you know, he was not personally acquainted with all the children and grandchildren of his many brothers and sisters. Salmon's sons, for instance, were perfect strangers to him, and all those boys and girls of the Evans' branch have never been long enough this side of the mountains for him to know their names, much less their temper or their lives. Yet his heirs—or such was his wish, his great wish—must be honest men, righteous in their dealings, and of stainless lives. If therefore, any one among you feels that for reasons he need not state, he has no right to accept his share of Anthony Westonhaugh's bounty, then that person is requested to withdraw before this letter to his heirs is read."

Withdraw? Was the man a fool? *Withdraw?*—these cormorants! these suckers of blood! these harpies and vultures! I laughed as I imagined sneaking Hector, malicious Luke or brutal John responding to this naïve appeal, and then found myself wondering why no echo of my mirth came from the men themselves. They must have seen much more plainly than I did the ludicrousness of their weak old kinsman's demand; yet Luke was still; Hector was still; and even John, and the three or four others I have mentioned gave forth no audible token of disdain or surprise. I was asking myself what sentiment of awe or fear restrained these selfish souls, when I became conscious of a movement within, which presently resolved itself into a departing footstep.

Some conscience there had been awakened. Some one was crossing the floor toward the door. Who? I waited in anxious expectancy for the word which was to enlighten me. Happily it came soon, and from the old lawyer's lips.

"You do not feel yourself worthy?" he queried, in tones I had not heard from him before. "Why? What have you done that you should forego an inheritance to which these others feel themselves honestly entitled?"

The voice which answered gave both my mind and heart a shock. It was *she* who had risen at this call. *She*, the only true-faced person there!

Anxiously I listened for her reply. Alas! it was one of action rather than speech. As I afterward heard, she simply opened her long cloak and showed a little infant slumbering in her arms.

"This is my reason," said she. "I have sinned in the eyes of the world, therefore I can not take my share of Uncle Anthony's money. I did not know he exacted an unblemished record from those he expected to enrich, or I would not have come."

The sob which followed these last words showed at what a cost she thus renounced a fortune of which she, of all present, perhaps, stood in the greatest need; but there was no lingering in her step; and to me, who understood her fault only through the faint sound of infantile wailing which accompanied her departure, there was a nobility in her action which raised her in an instant to an almost ideal height of unselfish virtue.

Perhaps they felt this, too. Perhaps even these hardened men and the more than hardened woman whose presence was in itself a blight, recognized heroism when they saw it; for when the lawyer, with a certain obvious reluctance, laid his hand on the bolts of the door with the remark: "This is not my work, you know; I am but following out instructions very minutely given me," the smothered growls and grunts which rose in reply lacked the venom which had been infused into all their previous comments.

"I think our friends out there are far enough withdrawn, by this time, for us to hazard the opening of the door," the lawyer now remarked. "Madam, I hope you will speedily find your way to some comfortable shelter."

Then the door opened, and after a moment, closed again in a silence which at least was respectful. Yet I warrant there was not a soul remaining who had not already figured in his mind to what extent his own fortune had been increased by the failure of one of their number to inherit.

As for me, my whole interest in the affair was at an end, and I was only anxious to find my way to where this desolate woman faced the mist with her unfed baby in her arms.

III

A LIFE DRAMA

But to reach this wanderer, it was first necessary for me to escape from the house. This proved simple enough. The up-stairs room toward which I rushed had a window overlooking one of the many lean-tos already mentioned. This window was fastened, but I had no difficulty in unlocking it or in finding my way to the ground from the top of the lean-to. But once again on terra-firma, I discovered that the mist was now so thick that it had all the effect of a fog at sea. It was icy cold as well, and clung about me so that I presently began to shudder most violently, and, strong man though I was, wish myself back in the little attic bedroom from which I had climbed in search of one in more unhappy case than myself.

But these feelings did not cause me to return. If I found the night cold, she must find it bitter. If desolation oppressed my naturally hopeful spirit, must it not be more overwhelming yet to one whose memories were sad and whose future was doubtful? And the child! What infant could live in an air like this! Edging away from the house, I called out her name, but no answer came back. The persons whom we had heard flitting in restless longing about the house a few moments before had left in rage and she, possibly, with them. Yet I could not imagine her joining herself to people of their stamp. There had been a solitariness in her aspect which seemed to forbid any such companionship. Whatever her story, at least she had nothing in common with the two ill-favored persons whose faces I had seen looking in at the casement. No; I should find her alone, but where? Certainly the ring of mist, surrounding me at that moment, offered me little prospect of finding her anywhere, either easily or soon.

Again I raised my voice, and again I failed to meet with response. Then, fearing to leave the house lest I should be quite lost amid the fences and brush lying between it and the road, I began to feel my way along the walls, calling softly now, instead of loudly, so anxious was I not to miss any chance of carrying comfort, if not succor, to the woman I was seeking. But the night gave back no sound, and when I came to the open door of a shed, I welcomed the refuge it offered and stepped in. I was, of course, confronted by darkness,—a different darkness from that without, blanket-like and impenetrable. But when after a moment of intense listening I heard a soft sound as of weariful breathing, I was seized anew by hope, and, feeling in my pocket for my match-box, I made a light and looked around.

My intuitions had not deceived me; she was there. Sitting on the floor with her cheek pressed against the wall, she revealed to my eager scrutiny only the outlines of her pure, pale profile; but in those outlines and on those pure, pale features, I saw such an abandonment of hope, mingled with such quiet endurance, that my whole soul melted before it, and it was with difficulty I managed to say:

"Pardon! I do not wish to intrude; but I am shut out of the house also; and the night is raw and cold. Can I do nothing for your comfort or for—for the child's?"

She turned toward me and I saw a tremulous gleam of pleasure disturb the somber stillness of her face; then the match went out in my hand, and we were again in complete darkness. But the little wail, which at the same instant rose from between her arms, filled up the pause, as her sweet "Hush!" filled my heart.

"I am used to the cold," came in another moment from the place where she crouched. "It is the child—she is hungry; and I—I walked here—feeling, hoping that, as my father's heir, I might partake in some slight measure of Uncle Anthony's money. Though my father cast me out before he died, and I have neither home nor money, I do not complain. I forfeited all when—" another wail, another gentle "hush!"—then silence.

I lit another match. "Look in my face!" I prayed. "I am a stranger, and you would be showing only proper prudence not to trust me. But I overheard your words when you withdrew from the room where your fortune lay; and I honor you, madam. If food can be got for your little one, I will get it."

I caught sight of the convulsive clasp with which she drew to her breast the tiny bundle she held, then darkness fell again.

"A little bread," she entreated; "a little milk—ah, baby, baby, hush!"

"But where can I get it?" I cried. "They are at table inside. I hear them shouting over their good cheer. But perhaps there are neighbors near by; do you know?"

"There are no neighbors," she replied. "What is got must be got here. I know a way to the kitchen; I used to visit Uncle Anthony when a little child; if you have the courage—"

I laughed. This token of confidence seemed to reassure her. I heard her move; possibly she stood up.

"In the further corner of this shed," said she, "there used to be a trap, connecting this floor with an underground passageway. A ladder stood against the trap, and the small cellar at the foot communicated by means of an iron-bound door with the large one under the house. Eighteen years ago the wood of that door was old; now it should be rotten. If you have the strength—"

"I will make the effort and see," said I. "But when I am in the cellar, what then?"

"Follow the wall to the right; you will come to a stone staircase. As this staircase has no railing, be careful in ascending it. At the top you will find a door; it leads into a pantry adjoining the kitchen. Some one will be in that pantry. Some one will give you a bite for the child; and when she is quieted and the sun has risen, I will go away. It is my duty to do so. My uncle was always upright, if cold. He was perfectly justified in exacting rectitude in his heirs."

I might have rejoined by asking if she detected rectitude in the faces of the greedy throng she had left behind her with the guardian of this estate; but I did not. I was too intent upon following out her directions. Lighting another match, I sought the trap. Alas! it was burdened with a pile of sticks and rubbish which looked as if they had lain there for years. As these had to be removed in total darkness, it took me some time. But once this debris had been scattered and thrown aside, I had no difficulty in finding the trap and, as the ladder was still there, I was soon on the cellar-bottom. When, by the reassuring shout I gave, she knew that I had advanced thus far, she spoke, and her voice had a soft and thrilling sound.

"Do not forget your own needs," she said. "We two are not so hungry that we can not wait for you to take a mouthful. I will sing to the baby. Good-by."

These ten minutes we had spent together had made us friends. The warmth, the strength which this discovery brought, gave to my arm a force that made that old oak door go down before me in three vigorous pushes.

Had the eight fortunate ones above not been indulging in a noisy celebration of their good luck, they must have heard the clatter of this door when it fell. But good eating, good drink, and the prospect of an immediate fortune far beyond their wildest dreams, made all ears deaf; and no pause occurred in the shouts of laughter and the hum of good-fellowship which sifted down between the beams supporting the house above my head. Consequently little or no courage was required for the completion of my adventure; and before long I came upon the staircase and the door leading from its top into the pantry. The next minute I was in front of that door.

But here a surprise awaited me. The noise which had hitherto been loud now became deafening, and I realized that, contrary to Eunice Westonhaugh's expectation, the supper had been spread in the kitchen and that I was likely to run amuck of the whole despicable crowd in any effort I might make to get a bite for the famished baby.

I therefore naturally hesitated to push open the door, fearing to draw attention to myself; and when I did succeed in lifting the latch and making a small crack, I was so astonished by the sudden lull in the general babble, that I drew hastily back and was for descending the stairs in sudden retreat.

But I was prevented from carrying out this cowardly impulse, by catching the sound of the lawyer's voice, addressing the assembled guests.

"You have eaten and you have drunk," he was saying; "you are therefore ready for the final toast. Brothers, nephews—heirs all of Anthony Westonhaugh, I rise to propose the name of your generous benefactor, who, if spirits walk this earth, must certainly be with us to-night."

A grumble from more than one throat and an uneasy hitch from such shoulders as I could see through my narrow vantage-hole testified to the rather doubtful pleasure with which this suggestion was received. But the lawyer's tones lost none of their animation as he went on to say:

"The bottle, from which your glasses are to be replenished for this final draft, he has himself provided. So anxious was he that it should be of the very best and altogether worthy of the occasion it is to celebrate, that he gave into my charge, almost with his dying breath, this key, telling me that it would unlock a cupboard here in which he had placed a bottle of wine of the very rarest vintage. This is the key, and yonder, if I do not mistake, is the cupboard."

They had already quaffed a dozen toasts. Perhaps this was why they accepted this proposition in a sort of panting silence, which remained unbroken while the lawyer crossed the floor, unlocked the cupboard and brought out before them a bottle which he held up before their eyes with a simulated glee almost saturnine.

"Isn't that a bottle to make your eyes dance? The very cobwebs on it are eloquent. And see! look at this label. Tokay, friends, real Tokay! How many of you ever had the opportunity of drinking real Tokay before?"

A long deep sigh from a half-dozen throats in which some strong but hitherto repressed passion, totally incomprehensible to me, found sudden vent, rose in one simultaneous sound from about that table, and I heard one jocular voice sing out:

"Pass it around, Smead. I'll drink to Uncle Anthony out of that bottle till there isn't a drop left to tell what was in it!"

But the lawyer was in no hurry.

"You have forgotten the letter, for the hearing of which you are called together. Mr. Anthony Westonhaugh left behind him a letter. The time is now come for reading it."

As I heard these words and realized that the final toast was to be delayed and that some few moments must yet elapse before the room would be cleared and an opportunity given me for obtaining what I needed for the famishing mother and child, I felt such impatience with the fact and so much anxiety as to the condition of those I had left behind me that I questioned whether it would not be better for me to return to them empty-handed than to leave them so long without the comfort of my presence, when the fascination of the scene again seized me and I found myself lingering to mark its conclusion with an avidity which can only be explained by my sudden and intense consciousness of what it all might mean to her whose witness I had thus inadvertently become.

The careful lawyer began by quoting the injunction with which this letter had been put in his hands. "'When they are warm with food and wine, but not too warm,'—thus his adjuration ran, 'then let them hear my first and only words to them.' I know you are eager for these words. Folk so honest, so convinced of their own purity and uprightness that they can stand unmoved while the youngest and most helpless among them withdraws her claim to wealth and independence rather than share an unmerited bounty, such folk, I say, must be eager, must be anxious to know why they have been made the legatees of so great a fortune, under the easy conditions and amid such slight restrictions as have been imposed upon them by their munificent kinsman."

"I had rather go on drinking toasts," babbled one thick voice.

"I had rather finish my figuring," growled another, in whose grating tones no echo remained of Hector Westonhaugh's formerly honeyed voice. "I am making out a list of stock—"

"Blast your stock! that is, if you mean horses and cows!" screamed a third. "I'm going in for city life. With less money than we have got, Andreas Amsberger got to be alderman—"

"Alderman!" sneered the whole pack; and the tumult became general. "If more of us had been sick," called out one; "or if Uncle Luke, say, had tripped into the ditch instead of on the edge of it, the fellows who came safe through might have had anything they wanted, even to the governorship of the state or—or—"

"Silence!" came in commanding tones from the lawyer, who had begun to let his disgust appear, perhaps because he held under his thumb the bottle upon which all eyes were now lovingly centered; so lovingly, indeed, that I ventured to increase, in the smallest perceptible degree, the crack by means of which I was myself an interested, if unseen, participator in this scene.

A sight of Smead, and a partial glimpse of old Luke's covetous profile, rewarded this small act of daring on my part. The lawyer was standing; all the rest were sitting. Perhaps he alone retained sufficient steadiness to stand; for I observed by the control he exercised over this herd of self-seekers, that he alone had not touched the cup which had so freely gone about among the others. The woman was hidden from me, but the change in her voice, when by any chance I heard it, convinced me that she had not disdained the toasts drunk by her brothers and nephews.

"Silence!" the lawyer reiterated, "or I will smash this bottle on the hearth." He raised it in one threatening hand and every man there seemed to tremble, while old Luke put out his long fingers with an entreaty that ill became them. "You want to hear the letter?" old Smead called out. "I thought so."

Putting the bottle down again, but still keeping one hand upon it, he drew a folded paper from his breast. "This," said he, "contains the final injunctions of Anthony Westonhaugh. You will listen, all of you; listen till I am done; or I will not only smash this bottle before your eyes, but I will keep for ever buried in my breast the whereabouts of certain drafts and bonds in which, as his heirs, you possess the greatest interest. Nobody but myself knows where these papers can be found."

Whether this was so, or whether the threat was an empty one thrown out by this subtle old schemer for the purpose of safeguarding his life from their possible hate and impatience, it answered his end with these semi-intoxicated men, and secured him the silence he demanded. Breaking open the seal of the envelope he held, he showed them the folded sheet which it contained, with the remark:

"I have had nothing to do with the writing of this letter. It is in Mr. Westonhaugh's own hand, and he was not even so good as to communicate to me the nature of its contents. I was bidden to read it to such as should be here assembled under the provisos mentioned in his will; and as you are now in a condition to listen, I will proceed with my task as required."

This was my time for leaving, but a certain brooding terror, latent in the air, held me chained to the spot, listening with my ears, but receiving the full sense of what was read from the expression of old Luke's face, which was probably more plainly visible to me than to those who sat beside him. For, being bent almost into a bow, as I have said, his forehead came within an inch of touching his plate, and one had to look under his arms, as I did, to catch the workings of his evil mouth, as old Smead gave forth, in his professional sing-song, the following words from his departed client:

"Brothers, nephews and heirs! Though the earth has lain upon my breast a month, I am with you here to-night."

A snort from old Luke's snarling lips; and a stir—not a comfortable one—in the jostling crowd, whose shaking arms and clawing hands I could see projecting here and there over the board.

"My presence at this feast—a presence which, if unseen, can not be unfelt, may bring you more pain than pleasure. But if so, it matters little. You are my natural heirs and I have left you my money; why, when so little love has characterized our intercourse, must be evident to such of my brothers as can recall their youth and the promise our father exacted from us on the day we set foot in this new land.

"There were nine of us in those days: Luke, Salmon, Barbara, Hector, Eustace, Janet, Hudson, William and myself; and all save one were promising, in appearance at least. But our father knew his offspring, and when we stood, an alien and miserable band in front of Castle Garden, at the foot of the great city whose immensity struck terror to our hearts, he drew all our hands together and made us swear by the soul of our mother, whose body we had left in the sea, that we would keep the bond of brotherhood intact, and share with mutual confidence whatever good fortune this untried country might hold in store for us. You were strong and your voices rang out loudly. Mine was faint, for I was weak—so weak that my hand had to be held in place by my sister Barbara. But my oath has never lost its hold upon my heart, while yours—answer how you have kept it, Luke; or you, Janet; or you Hector, of the smooth tongue and vicious heart; or you, or you, who, from one stock, recognize but one law: the law of cold-blooded selfishness which seeks its own in face of all oaths and at the cost of another man's heart-break.

"This I say to such as know my story. But lest there be one amongst you who has not heard from parent or uncle the true tale of him who has brought you all under one roof to-night, I will repeat it here in words, that no man may fail to understand why I remembered my oath through life and beyond death, yet stand above you an accusing spirit while you quaff me toasts and count the gains my justice divides among you.

"I, as you all remember, was the weak one—the ne'er-do-weel. When all of you were grown and had homes of your own, I still remained under the family roof-tree, fed by our father's bounty and looking to our father's justice for that share of his savings which he had promised to all alike. When he died it came to me as it came to you; but I had married before that day; married, not, like the rest of you, for what a wife could bring, but for sentiment and true passion. This, in my case, meant a loving wife, but a frail one; and while we lived a little while on the patrimony left us, it was far too small to support us long without some aid from our own hands; and our hands were feeble and could not work. And so we fell into debt for rent and, ere long, for the commonest necessities of life. In vain I struggled to redeem myself; the time of my prosperity had not come and I only sank deeper and deeper into debt and finally into indigence. A baby came. Our landlord was kind and allowed us to stay for two weeks under the roof for whose protection we could not pay; but at the end of that time we were asked to leave; and I found myself on the road with a dying wife, a wailing infant, no money in my purse and no power in my arm to earn any. Then when heart and hope were both failing, I recalled that ancient oath and the six prosperous homes scattered up and down the very highway on which I stood. I could not leave my wife; the fever was in her veins and she could not bear me out of her sight; so I put her on a horse, which a kind old neighbor was willing to lend me, and holding her up with one hand, guided the horse with the other, to the home of my brother Luke. He was a straight enough fellow in those days—physically, I mean—and he looked able and strong that morning, as he stood in the open doorway of his house, gazing down at us as we halted before him in the roadway. But his temper had grown greedy with the accumulation of a few dollars, and he shook his head as he closed his door, saying he remembered no oath and that spenders must expect to be beggars.

"Struck to the heart by a rebuff which meant prolongation of the suffering I saw in my dear wife's eyes, I stretched up and kissed her where she sat half-fainting on the horse; then I moved on. I came to Barbara's home next. She had been a little mother to me once; that is, she had fed and dressed me, and doled out blows and caresses, and taught me to read and sing. But Barbara in her father's home and without fortune was not the Barbara I saw on the threshold of the little cottage she called her own. She heard my story; looked in the face of my wife and turned her back. She had no place for idle folk in her little house; if we would work she would feed us; but we must earn our supper or go hungry to bed. I felt the trembling of my wife's frame where she leaned against my arm, and kissing her again, led her on to Salmon's. Luke, Hector, Janet, have you heard him tell of that vision at his gateway, twenty-five years ago? He is not amongst you. For twelve years he has lain beside our father in the churchyard, but his sons may be here, for they were ever alert when gold was in sight or a full glass to be drained. Ask *them*, ask John, whom I saw skulking behind his cousins at the garden fence that day, what it was they saw as I drew rein under the great tree which shadowed their father's doorstep.

"The sunshine had been pitiless that morning, and the head, for whose rest in some loving shelter I would have bartered soul and body, had fallen sidewise till it lay on my arm. Pressed to her breast was our infant, whose little wail struck in pitifully as Salmon called out: 'What's to do here to-day!' Do you remember it, lads? or how you all laughed, little and great, when I asked for a few weeks' stay under my brother's roof till we could all get well and go about our tasks again? *I* remember. I, who am writing these words from the very mouth of the tomb, *I* remember; but I did not curse you. I only rode on to the next. The way ran uphill now; and the sun which, since our last stop, had been under a cloud, came out and blistered my wife's cheeks, already burning red with fever. But I pressed my lips upon them, and led her on. With each rebuff I gave her a kiss; and her smile, as her head pressed harder and harder upon my arm now exerting all its strength to support her, grew almost divine. But it vanished at my nephew Lemuel's.

"He was shearing sheep, and could give no time to company; and when, late in the day, I drew rein at Janet's, and she said she was going to have a dance and could not look after sick folk, the pallid lips failed to return my despairing embrace; and in the terror which this brought me I went down, in the gathering twilight, into the deep valley where William raised his sheep and reckoned, day by day, the increase among his pigs. Oh, the chill of that descent! Oh, the gloom of the gathering shadows! As we neared the bottom and I heard a far-off voice shout out a hoarse command, some instinct made me reach up for the last time and bestow that faithful kiss, which was at once her consolation and my prayer. My lips were cold with the terror of my soul, but they were not so cold as the cheek they touched, and, shrieking in my misery and need, I fell before William where he halted by the horse-trough and—He was always a hard man, was William, and it was a shock to him, no doubt, to see us standing in our anguish and necessity before him; but he raised the whip in his hand and, when it fell, my arm fell with it and she slipped from my grasp to the ground, and lay in a heap in the roadway.

"He was ashamed next minute and pointed to the house near-by. But I did not carry her in, and she died in the roadway. Do you remember it, Luke? Do you remember it, Lemuel?

"But it is not of this I complain at this hour, nor is it for this I ask you to drink the toast I have prepared for you."

The looks, the writhings of old Luke and such others as I could now see through the widening crack my hands unconsciously made in the doorway, told me that the rack was at work in this room so lately given up to revelry. Yet the mutterings, which from time to time came to my ears from one sullen lip or another, did not rise into frightened imprecation or even into any assertion of sorrow or contrition. It seemed as if some suspense, common to all, held them speechless if not dumbly apprehensive; and while the lawyer said nothing in recognition of this, he could not have been quite blind to it, for he bestowed one curious glance around the table before he proceeded with old Anthony's words.

Those words had now become short, sharp, and accusatory.

"My child lived; and what remained to me of human passion and longing centered in his frail existence. I managed to earn enough for his eating and housing, and in time I was almost happy again. This was while our existence was a struggle; but when, with the discovery of latent powers in my own mind, I began to find my place in the world and to earn money, then your sudden interest in my boy taught me a new lesson in human selfishness; but not, as yet, new fears. My nature was not one to grasp ideas of evil, and the remembrance of that oath still remained to make me lenient toward you.

"I let him see you; not much, not often, but yet often enough for him to realize that he had uncles and cousins, or, if you like it better, kindred. And how did you repay this confidence on my part? What hand had ye in the removal of this small barrier to the fortune my own poor health warranted you in looking upon, even in those early days, as your own? To others' eyes it may appear, none; to mine, ye are one and all his murderers, as certainly as all of you were the murderers of the good physician hastening to his aid. For his illness was not a mortal one. He would have been saved if the doctor had reached him; but a precipice swallowed that good Samaritan, and only I, of all who looked upon the footprints which harrowed up the road at this dangerous point, knew whose shoes would fit those marks. God's providence, it was called, and I let it pass for such; but it was a providence which cost me my boy and made *you* my heirs."

Silence as sullen in character as the men who found themselves thus openly impeached had, for some minutes now, replaced the muttered complaints which had accompanied the first portion of this denunciatory letter. As the lawyer stopped to cast them another of those strange looks, a gleam from old Luke's sidewise eyes startled the man next him, who, shrugging a shoulder, passed the underhanded look on, till it had circled the board and stopped with the man sitting opposite the crooked sinner who had started it.

I began to have a wholesome dread of them all and was astonished to see the lawyer drop his hand from the bottle, which to some degree offered itself as a possible weapon. But he knew his audience better than I did. Though the bottle was now free for any man's taking, not a hand trembled toward it, nor was a single glass held out.

The lawyer, with an evil smile, went on with his relentless client's story.

"Ye had killed my wife; ye had killed my son; but this was not enough. Being lonesome in my great house, which was as much too large for me as my fortune was, I had taken a child to replace the boy I had lost. Remembering the cold blood running in the veins of those nearest me, I chose a boy from alien stock and, for a while, knew contentment again. But, as he developed and my affections strengthened, the possibility of all my money going his way roused my brothers and sisters from the complacency they had enjoyed since their road to fortune had been secured by my son's death, and one day—can you recall it, Hudson? can you recall it, Lemuel?—the boy was brought in from the mill and laid at my feet, dead! He had stumbled amongst the great belts, but whose was the voice which had startled him with a sudden 'Halloo!' Can you say, Luke? Can you say, John? I can say in whose ear it was whispered that three, if not more of you, were seen moving among the machinery that fatal morning.

"Again, God's providence was said to have visited my house; and again *ye* were my heirs."

"Stop there!" broke in the harsh voice of Luke, who was gradually growing livid under his long gray locks.

"Lies! lies!" shrieked Hector, gathering courage from his brother.

"Cut it all and give us the drink!" snarled one of the younger men, who was less under the effect of liquor than the rest.

But a trembling voice muttered "Hush!" and the lawyer, whose eye had grown steely under these comments, took advantage of the sudden silence which had followed this last objurgation and went steadily on.

"Some men would have made a will and denounced you. I made a will, but did not denounce you. *I* am no breaker of oaths. More than this, I learned a new trick. I, who hated all subtlety and looked upon craft as the favorite weapon of the devil, learned to smile with my lips while my heart was burning with hatred. Perhaps this was why you all began to smile too, and joke me about certain losses I had sustained, by which you meant the gains which had come to me. That these gains were many times greater than you realized added to the sting of this good fellowship, but I held my peace; and you began to have confidence in a good-nature which nothing could shake. You even gave me a supper."

A supper!

What was there in these words to cause every man there to stop in whatever movement he was making and stare, with wide-open eyes, intently at the reader. He had spoken quietly; he had not even looked up, but the silence which, for some minutes back, had begun to reign over that tumultuous gathering, now became breathless, and the seams in Hector's cheeks deepened to a bluish criss-cross.

"You remember that supper?"

As the words rang out again, I threw wide the door; I might have stalked openly into their circle; not a man there would have noticed me.

"It was a memorable occasion," the lawyer read on with stoical impassiveness. "There was not a brother lacking. Luke and Hudson and William and Hector and Eustace's boys, as well as Eustace himself; Janet too, and Salmon's Lemuel, and Barbara's son, who, even if his mother had gone the way of all flesh, had so trained her black brood in the love of the things of this world that I scarcely missed her when I looked about among you all for the eight sturdy brothers and sisters who had joined in one clasp and one oath, under the eye of the true-hearted immigrant, our father. What I did miss was one true eye lifted to my glance; but I did not show that I missed it; and so our peace was made and we separated, you to wait for your inheritance, and I for the death which was to secure it to you. For, when the cup passed round that night, you each dropped into it a tear of repentance, and tears make bitter drinking. I sickened as I quaffed and was never myself again, as you know. Do you understand me, you cruel, crafty ones?"

Did they not! Heads quaking, throats gasping, teeth chattering—no longer sitting—all risen, all looking with wild eyes for the door—was it not apparent that they understood and only waited for one more word to break away and flee the accursed house?

But that word lingered. Old Smead had now grown pale himself and read with difficulty the lines which were to end this frightful scene. As I saw the red gleam of terror shine out from his small eyes, I wondered if he had been but the blind tool of his implacable client and was as ignorant as those before him of what was to follow this heavy arraignment. The dread with which he finally proceeded was too marked for me to doubt the truth of this surmise. This is what he found himself forced to read:

"There was a bottle reserved for me. It had a green label on it, —"

A shriek from every one there and a hurried look up and down at the bottles standing on the table.

"A green label," the lawyer repeated, "and it made a goodly appearance as it was set down before me. But you had no liking for wine with a green label on the bottle. One by one you refused it, and when I rose to quaff my final glass alone, every eye before me fell and did not lift again until the glass was drained. I did not notice this then, but I see it all now, just as I hear again the excuses you gave for not filling your glasses as the bottle went round. One had drunk enough; one suffered from qualms brought on by an unaccustomed indulgence in oysters; one felt that wine good enough for me was too good for him, and so on and so on. Not one to show frank eyes and drink with me as I was ready to drink with him! Why? Because one and all of you knew what was in that cup, and would not risk an inheritance so nearly within your grasp."

"Lies! lies!" again shrieked the raucous voice of Luke, smothered by terror; while oaths, shouts, imprecations, rang out in horrid tumult from one end of the table to the other, till the lawyer's face, over which a startling change was rapidly passing, drew the whole crowd forward again in awful fascination, till they clung, speechless, arm in arm, shoulder propping shoulder, while he gasped out in dismay equal to their own, these last fatal words:

"That was at your board, my brothers; now you are at mine. You have eaten my viands, drunk of my cup; and now, through the mouth of the one man who has been true to me because therein lies his advantage, I offer you a final glass. Will you drink it? I drank yours. By that old-time oath which binds us to share each other's fortune, I ask you to share this cup with me. *You will not?*"

"No, no, no!" shouted one after another.

"Then," the inexorable voice went on, a voice which to these miserable souls was no longer that of the lawyer, but an issue from the grave they had themselves dug for Anthony Westonhaugh, "know that your abstinence comes too late; that you have already drunk the toast destined to end your lives. The bottle which you must have missed from that board of yours has been offered you again. A label is easily changed and—Luke, John, Hector, I know you all so well—that bottle has been greedily emptied by you; and while I, who sipped sparingly, lived three weeks, you, who have drunk deep, *have not three hours before you, possibly not three minutes.*"

O, the wail of those lost souls as this last sentence issued in a final pant of horror from the lawyer's quaking lips! Shrieks—howls—prayers for mercy—groans to make the hair rise—and curses, at sound of which I shut my ears in horror, only to open them again in dread as, with one simultaneous impulse, they flung themselves upon the lawyer who, foreseeing this rush, had backed up against the wall.

He tried to stem the tide.

"I knew nothing of the poisoning," he protested. "That was not my reason for declining the drink. I wished to preserve my senses—to carry out my client's wishes. As God lives, I did not know he meant to carry his revenge so far. Mercy! Mer—"

But the hands which clutched him were the hands of murderers, and the lawyer's puny figure could not stand up against the avalanche of human terror, relentless fury and mad vengeance which now rolled in upon it. As I bounded to his relief he turned his ghastly face upon me. But the way between us was blocked, and I was preparing myself to see him sink before my eyes, when an unearthly shriek rose from behind us, and every living soul in that mass of struggling humanity paused, set and staring, with stiffened limbs and eyes fixed, not on him, not on me, but on one of their own number, the only woman amongst them, Janet Clapsaddle, who, with clutching hands clawing her breast, was reeling in solitary agony in her place beside the board. As they looked she fell, and lay with upturned face and staring eyes, in whose glassy depths the ill-fated ones who watched her could see mirrored their own impending doom.

It was an awful moment. A groan, in which was concentrated the despair of seven miserable souls, rose from that petrified band; then, man by man, they separated and fell back, showing on each weak or wicked face the particular passion which had driven them into crime and made them the victims of this wholesale revenge. There had been some sort of bond between them till the vision of death rose before each shrinking soul. Shoulder to shoulder in crime, they fell apart as their doom approached; and rushing, shrieking, each man for himself, they one and all sought to escape by doors, windows or any outlet which promised release from this fatal spot. One rushed by me—I do not know which one—and I felt as if a flame from hell had licked me, his breath was so hot and the moans he uttered so like the curses we imagine to blister the lips of the lost. None of them saw me; they did not even detect the sliding form of the lawyer crawling away before them to some place of egress of which they had no knowledge; and, convinced that in this scene of death I could play no part worthy of her who awaited me, I too rushed away and, groping my way back through the cellar, sought the side of her who still crouched in patient waiting against the dismal wall.

IV

THE FINAL SHOCK

Her baby had fallen asleep. I knew this by the faint, low sweetness of her croon; and, shuddering with the horrors I had witnessed, horrors which acquired a double force from the contrast presented by the peace of this quiet spot and the hallowing influence of the sleeping infant,—I threw myself down in the darkness at her feet, gasping out:

"Oh, thank God and your uncle's seeming harshness, that you have escaped the doom which has overtaken those others! You and your babe are still alive; while they—"

"What of them? What has happened to them? You are breathless, trembling; you have brought no bread—"

"No, no. Food in this house means death. Your relatives gave food and wine to your uncle at a supper; he, though now in his grave, has returned the same to them. There was a bottle—"

I stopped, appalled. A shriek, muffled by distance but quivering with the same note of death I had heard before, had gone up again from the other side of the wall against which we were leaning.

"Oh!" she gasped; "and my father was at that supper! my father, who died last night cursing the day he was born! We are an accursed race. I have known it all my life; perhaps that was why I mistook passion for love; and my baby—O God, have mercy! God have mercy!"

The plaintiveness of that cry, the awesomeness of what I had seen—of what was going on at that moment almost within the reach of our arms—the darkness, the desolation of our two souls, affected me as I had never been affected in my whole life before. In the concentrated experience of the last two hours I seemed to live years under this woman's eyes; to know her as I did my own heart; to love her as I did my own soul. No growth of feeling ever brought the ecstasy of that moment's inspiration. With no sense of doing anything strange, with no fear of being misunderstood, I reached out my hand and, touching hers where it lay clasped about her infant, I said:

"We are two poor wayfarers. A rough road loses half its difficulties when trodden by two. Shall we, then, fare on together—we and the little child?"

She gave a sob; there was sorrow, longing, grief, hope, in its thrilling low sound. As I recognized the latter emotion I drew her to my breast. The child did not separate us.

"We shall be happy," I murmured, and her sigh seemed to answer a delicious "Yes," when suddenly there came a shock to the partition against which we leaned and, starting from my clasp, she cried:

"Our duty is in there. Shall we think of ourselves or even of each other while these men, all relatives of mine, are dying on the other side of this wall?"

Seizing my hand, she dragged me to the trap; but here I took the lead, and helped her down the ladder. When I had her safely on the floor at the foot, she passed in front of me again; but once up the steps and in front of the kitchen door, I thrust her behind me, for one glance into the room beyond had convinced me it was no place for her.

But she would not be held back. She crowded forward beside me, and together we looked upon the wreck within. It was a never-to-be-forgotten scene. The demon that was in those men had driven them to demolish furniture, dishes, everything. In one heap lay what, an hour before, had been an inviting board surrounded by rollicking and greedy guests. But it was not upon this overthrow we stopped to look. It was upon something that mingled with it, dominated it and made of this chaos only a setting to awful death. Janet's face, in all its natural hideousness and depravity, looked up from the floor beside this heap; and farther on, the twisted figure of him they called Hector, with something more than the seams of greedy longing round his wide, staring eyes and icy temples. Two in this room! and on the threshold of the one beyond a moaning third, who sank into eternal silence as we approached; and before the fireplace in the great room, a horrible crescent that had once been aged Luke, upon whom we had no sooner turned our backs than we caught glimpses here and there of other prostrate forms which moved once under our eyes and then moved no more.

One only still stood upright, and he was the man whose obtrusive figure and sordid expression had so revolted me in the beginning. There was no color now in his flabby and heavily fallen cheeks. The eyes, in whose false sheen I had seen so much of evil, were glazed now, and his big and burly frame shook the door it pressed against. He was staring at a small slip of paper he held, and, from his anxious looks, appeared to miss something which neither of us had power to supply. It was a spectacle to make devils rejoice, and mortals fly aghast. But Eunice had a spirit like an angel and drawing near him, she said:

"Is there anything I can do for you, Cousin John?"

He started, looked at her with the same blank gaze he had hitherto cast at the wall; then some words formed on his working lips and we heard:

"I can not reckon; I was never good at figures; but if Luke is gone, and William, and Hector, and Barbara's boy, and Janet, —*how much does that leave for me?*"

He was answered almost the moment he spoke; but it was by other tongues and in another world than this. As his body fell forward, I tore open the door before which he had been standing, and, lifting the almost fainting Eunice in my arms, I carried her out into the night. As I did so, I caught a final glimpse of the pictured face I had found it so hard to understand a couple of hours before. I understood it now.

A surprise awaited us as we turned toward the gate. The mist had lifted and a keen but not unpleasant wind was driving from the north. Borne on it, we heard voices. The village had emptied itself, probably at the alarm given by the lawyer, and it was these good men and women whose approach we heard. As we had nothing to fear from them, we went forward to meet them. As we did so, three crouching figures rose from some bushes we passed and ran scurrying before us through the gateway. They were the late comers who had shown such despair at being shut out from this fatal house, and who probably did not yet know the doom they had escaped.

There were lanterns in the hands of some of the men who now approached. As we stopped before them, these lanterns were held up, and by the light they gave we saw, first, the lawyer's frightened face, then the visages of two men who seemed to be persons of some authority.

"What news?" faltered the lawyer, seeing by our faces that we knew the worst.

"Bad," I returned; "the poison had lost none of its virulence by being mixed so long with the wine."

"How many?" asked the man on his right anxiously.

"Eight," was my solemn reply.

"There were but eight," faltered the lawyer; "that means, then, all?"

"All," I repeated.

A murmur of horror rose, swelled, then died out in tumult as the crowd swept on past us.

For a moment we stood watching these people; saw them pause before the door we had left open behind us, then rush in, leaving a wail of terror on the shuddering midnight air. When all was quiet again, Eunice laid her hand upon my arm.

"Where shall we go?" she asked despairingly. "I do not know a house that will open to me."

The answer to her question came from other lips than mine.

"I do not know one that will *not*," spoke up a voice behind our backs. "Your withdrawal from the circle of heirs did not take from you your rightful claim to an inheritance which, according to your uncle's will, could be forfeited only by a failure to arrive at the place of distribution within the hour set by the testator. As I see the matter now, this appeal to the honesty of the persons so collected was a test by which my unhappy client strove to save from the general fate such members of his miserable family as fully recognized their sin and were truly repentant."

It was Lawyer Smead. He had lingered behind the others to tell her this. She was, then, no outcast, but rich, very rich; how rich I dared not acknowledge to myself, lest a remembrance of the man who was the last to perish in that house of death should return to make this calculation hateful. It was a blow which struck deep, deeper than any either of us had sustained that night. As we came to realize it, I stepped slowly back, leaving her standing erect and tall in the middle of the roadway, with her baby in her arms. But not for long; soon she was close at my side murmuring softly:

"Two wayfarers still! Only, the road will be more difficult and the need of companionship greater. Shall we fare on together, you, I—and the little one?"

THE RUBY AND THE CALDRON

THE RUBY AND THE CALDRON

As there were two good men on duty that night, I did not see why I should remain at my desk, even though there was an unusual stir created in our small town by the grand ball given at The Evergreens.

But just as I was preparing to start for home, an imperative ring called me to the telephone and I heard:

"Halloo! Is this the police-station?"

"It is."

"Well, then, a detective is wanted at once at The Evergreens. He can not be too clever or too discreet. A valuable jewel has been lost, which must be found before the guests disperse for home. Large reward if the matter ends successfully and without too great publicity."

"May I ask who is speaking to me?"

"Mrs. Ashley."

It was the mistress of The Evergreens and giver of the ball.

"Madam, a man shall be sent at once. Where will you see him?"

"In the butler's pantry at the rear. Let him give his name as Jennings."

"Very good. Good-by."

"Good-by."

A pretty piece of work! Should I send Hendricks or should I send Hicks? Hendricks was clever and Hicks discreet, but neither united both qualifications in the measure demanded by the sensible and quietly-resolved woman with whom I had just been talking. What alternative remained? But one; I must go myself.

It was not late—not for a ball night, at least—and as half the town had been invited to the dance, the streets were alive with carriages. I was watching the blink of their lights through the fast falling snow when my attention was drawn to a fact which struck me as peculiar. These carriages were all coming my way instead of rolling in the direction of The Evergreens. Had they been empty this would have needed no explanation, but, as far as I could see, most of them were full, and that, too, with loudly talking women and gesticulating men.

Something of a serious nature must have occurred at The Evergreens. Rapidly I paced on and soon found myself before the great gates.

A crowd of vehicles of all descriptions blocked the entrance. None seemed to be passing up the driveway; all stood clustered at the gates, and as I drew nearer I perceived many an anxious head thrust forth from their quickly opened doors and heard many an ejaculation of disappointment as the short interchange of words went on between the drivers of these various turnouts and a man drawn up in quiet resolution before the unexpectedly barred entrance.

Slipping round to this man's side, I listened to what he was saying. It was simple but very explicit.

"Mrs. Ashley asks everybody's pardon, but the ball can't go on to-night. Something has happened which makes the reception of further guests impossible. To-morrow evening she will be happy to see you all. The dance is simply post-poned."

This he had probably repeated forty times, and each time it had probably been received with the same mixture of doubt and curiosity which now held the lengthy procession in check.

Not wishing to attract attention, yet anxious to lose no time, I pressed up still nearer, and, bending toward him from the shadow cast by a convenient post, uttered the one word:

"Jennings."

Instantly he unlocked a small gate at his right. I passed in and, with professional *sang-froid*, proceeded to take my way to the house through the double row of evergreens bordering the semicircular approach.

As these trees stood very close together and were, besides, heavily laden with fresh-fallen snow, I failed to catch a glimpse of the building itself until I stood in front of it. Then I saw that it was brilliantly lighted and gave evidence here and there of some festivity; but the guests were too few for the effect to be very exhilarating and, passing around to the rear, I sought the special entrance to which I had been directed.

A heavy-browed porch, before which stood a caterer's wagon, led me to a door which had every appearance of being the one I sought. Pushing it open, I entered without ceremony, and speedily found myself in the midst of twenty or more colored waiters and chattering housemaids. To one of the former I addressed the question:

"Where is the butler's pantry? I am told that I shall find the lady of the house there."

"Your name?" was the curt demand.

"Jennings."

"Follow me."

I was taken through narrow passages and across one or two store-rooms to a small but well-lighted closet, where I was left, with the assurance that Mrs. Ashley would presently join me. I had never seen this lady, but I had often heard her spoken of as a woman of superior character and admirable discretion.

She did not keep me waiting. In two minutes the door opened and this fine, well-poised woman was telling her story in the straight-forward manner I so much admire and so seldom meet with.

The article lost was a large ruby of singular beauty and great value—the property of Mrs. Burton, the senator's wife, in whose honor this ball was given. It had not been lost in the house nor had it been originally missed that evening. Mrs. Burton and herself had attended the great foot-ball game in the afternoon, and it was on the college campus that Mrs. Burton had first dropped her invaluable jewel. But a reward of five hundred dollars having been at once offered to whoever should find and restore it, a great search had followed, which ended in its being picked up by one of the students and brought back as far as the great step leading up to the front door, when it had again disappeared, and in a way to rouse conjecture of the strangest and most puzzling character.

The young man who had brought it thus far bore the name of John Deane, and was a member of the senior class. He had been the first to detect its sparkle in the grass, and those who were near enough to see his face at that happy moment say that it expressed the utmost satisfaction at his good luck.

"You see," said Mrs. Ashley, "he has a sweetheart, and five hundred dollars looks like a fortune to a young man just starting life. But he was weak enough to take this girl into his confidence; and on their way here—for both were invited to the ball—he went so far as to pull it out of his pocket and show it to her.

"They were admiring it together and vaunting its beauties to the young lady friend who had accompanied them, when their carriage turned into the driveway and they saw the lights of the house flashing before them. Hastily restoring the jewel to the little bag he had made for it out of the finger-end of an old glove,—a bag in which he assured me he had been careful to keep it safely tied ever since picking it up on the college green,—he thrust it back into his pocket and prepared to help the ladies out. But just then a disturbance arose in front. A horse which had been driven up was rearing in a way that threatened to overturn the light buggy to which he was attached. As the occupants of this buggy were ladies, and seemed to have no control over the plunging beast, young Deane naturally sprang to the rescue. Bidding his own ladies alight and make for the porch, he hurriedly ran forward and, pausing in front of the maddened animal, waited for an opportunity to seize him by the rein. He says that as he stood there facing the beast with fixed eye and raised hand, he distinctly felt something strike or touch his breast. But the sensation conveyed no meaning to him in his excitement, and he did not think of it again till, the horse well in hand and the two alarmed occupants of the buggy rescued, he turned to see where his own ladies were, and beheld them looking down at him from the midst of a circle of young people, drawn from the house by the screaming of the women. Instantly a thought of the treasure he carried recurred to his mind, and dropping the rein of the now quieted horse, he put his hand to his pocket. The jewel was gone. He declares that for a moment he felt as if he had been struck on the head by one of the hoofs of the frantic horse he had just handled. But immediately the importance of his loss and the necessity he felt for instant action restored him to himself, and shouting aloud, 'I have dropped Mrs. Burton's ruby!'

begged every one to stand still while he made a search for it.

"This all occurred, as you must know, more than an hour and a half ago, consequently before many of my guests had arrived. My son, who was one of the few spectators gathered on the porch, tells me that there was only one other carriage behind the one in which Mr. Deane had brought his ladies. Both of these had stopped short of the stepping-stone, and as the horse and buggy which had made all this trouble had by this time been driven to the stable, nothing stood in the way of his search but the rapidly accumulating snow which, if you remember, was falling very thick and fast at the time.

"My son, who had rushed in for his overcoat, came running down with offers to help him. So did some others. But, with an imploring gesture, he begged to be allowed to conduct the search alone, the ground being in such a state that the delicately-mounted jewel ran great risk of being trodden into the snow and thus injured or lost. They humored him for a moment, then, seeing that his efforts bade fair to be fruitless, my son insisted upon joining him, and the two looked the ground over, inch by inch, from the place where Mr. Deane had set foot to ground in alighting from his carriage to the exact spot where he had stood when he had finally seized hold of the horse. But no ruby. Then Harrison (that is my son's name) sent for a broom and went over the place again, sweeping aside the surface snow and examining carefully the ground beneath,—but with no better results than before. No ruby could be found. My son came to me panting. Mrs. Burton and myself stood awaiting him in a state of suspense. Guests and fête were alike forgotten. We had heard that the jewel had been found on the campus by one of the students and had been brought back as far as the step in front and then lost again in some unaccountable manner in the snow, and we hoped, nay expected from moment to moment, that it would be brought in.

"When Harrison entered, then, pale, disheveled and shaking his head, Mrs. Burton caught me by the hand, and I thought she would faint. For this jewel is of far greater value to her than its mere worth in money, though that is by no means small.

"It is a family jewel and was given to her by her husband under special circumstances. He prizes it even more than she does, and he is not here to counsel or assist her in this extremity. Besides, she was wearing it in direct opposition to his expressed wishes. This I must tell you, to show how imperative it is for us to recover it; also to account for the large reward she is willing to pay. When he last looked at it he noticed that the fastening was a trifle slack and, though he handed the trinket back, he told her distinctly that she was not to wear it till it had been either to Tiffany's or Starr's. But she considered it safe enough, and put it on to please the boys, and lost it. Senator Burton is a hard man and,—in short, the jewel must be found. I give you just one hour in which to do it."

"But, madam—" I protested.

"I know," she put in, with a quick nod and a glance over her shoulder to see if the door was shut. "I have not finished my story. Hearing what Harrison had to say, I took action at once. I bade him call in the guests, whom curiosity or interest still detained on the porch, and seat them in a certain room which I designated to him. Then, after telling him to send two men to the gates with orders to hold back all further carriages from entering, and two others to shovel up and cart away to the stable every particle of snow for ten feet each side of the front step, I asked to see Mr. Deane. But here my son whispered something into my ear, which it is my duty to repeat. It was to the effect that Mr. Deane believed that the jewel had been taken from him; that he insisted, in fact, that he had felt a hand touch his breast while he stood awaiting an opportunity to seize the horse. 'Very good,' said I, 'we'll remember that, too; but first see that my orders are carried out and that all approaches to the grounds are guarded and no one allowed to come in or go out without permission from me.'

"He left us, and I was turning to encourage Mrs. Burton when my attention was caught by the eager face of a little friend of mine, who, quite unknown to me, was sitting in one of the corners of the room. She was studying my countenance in a sort of subdued anxiety, hardly natural in one so young, and I was about to call her to my side and question her when she made a sudden dive and vanished from the room. Some impulse made me follow her. She is a conscientious little thing, but timid as a hare, and though I saw she had something to say, it was with difficulty I could make her speak. Only after the most solemn assurances that her name should not be mentioned in the matter, would she give me the following bit of information, which you may possibly think throws another light upon the affair. It seems that she was looking out of one of the front windows when Mr. Deane's carriage drove up. She had been watching the antics of the horse attached to the buggy, but as soon as she saw Mr. Deane going to the assistance of those in danger, she let her eyes stray back to the ladies whom he had left behind him in the carriage.

"She did not know these ladies, but their looks and gestures interested her, and she watched them quite intently as they leaped to the ground and made their way toward the porch. One went on quickly, and without pause, to the step, but the other, —the one who came last, —did not do this. She stopped a moment, perhaps to watch the horse in front, perhaps to draw her cloak more closely about her, and when she again moved on, it was with a start and a hurried glance at her feet, terminating in a quick turn and a sudden stooping to the ground. When she again stood upright, she had something in her hand which she thrust furtively into her breast."

"How was this lady dressed?" I inquired.

"In a white cloak, with an edging of fur. I took pains to learn that, too, and it was with some curiosity, I assure you, that I examined the few guests who had now been admitted to the room I had so carefully pointed out to my son. Two of them wore white cloaks, but one of these was Mrs. Dalrymple, and I did not give her or her cloak a second thought. The other was a tall, fine-looking girl, with an air and bearing calculated to rouse admiration if she had not shown so very plainly that she was in a state of inner perturbation. Though she tried to look amiable and pleased, I saw that she had some care on her mind, which, had she been Mr. Deane's *fiancée*, would have needed no explanation; but as she was only Mr.

Deane's *fiancée's* friend, its cause was not so apparent.

"The floor of the room, as I had happily remembered, was covered with crash, and as I lifted each garment off—I allowed no maid to assist me in this—I shook it well; ostensibly, because of the few flakes clinging to it, really to see if anything could be shaken out of it. Of course, I met with no success. I had not expected to, but it is my disposition to be thorough. These wraps I saw all hung in an adjoining closet, the door of which I locked,—here is the key,—after which I handed my guests over to my son who led them into the drawing-room where they joined the few others who had previously arrived, and went myself to telephone to *you*."

I bowed and asked where the young people were now.

"Still in the drawing-room. I have ordered the musicians to play, and consequently there is more or less dancing. But, of course, nothing can remove the wet blanket which has fallen over us all,—nothing but the finding of this jewel. Do you see your way to accomplishing this? We are, from this very moment, at your disposal; only I pray that you will make no more disturbance than is necessary, and, if possible, arouse no suspicions you can not back up by facts. I dread a scandal almost as much as I do sickness and death, and these young people—well, their lives are all before them, and neither Mrs. Burton nor myself would wish to throw the shadow of a false suspicion over the least of them."

I assured her that I sympathized with her scruples and would do my best to recover the ruby without inflicting undue annoyance upon the innocent. Then I inquired whether it was known that a detective had been called in. She seemed to think it was suspected by some, if not by all. At which my way seemed a trifle complicated.

We were about to proceed when another thought struck me.

"Madam, you have not said whether the carriage itself was searched."

"I forgot. Yes, the carriage was thoroughly overhauled, and before the coachman left the box."

"Who did this overhauling?"

"My son. He would not trust any other hand than his own in a business of this kind."

"One more question, madam. Was any one seen to approach Mr. Deane on the carriage-drive prior to his assertion that the jewel was lost?"

"No. *And there were no tracks in the snow of any such person.* My son looked."

And I would look, or so I decided within myself, but I said nothing; and in silence we proceeded toward the drawing-room.

I had left my overcoat behind me, and always being well-dressed, I did not present so bad an appearance. Still I was not in party attire and naturally could not pass for a guest if I had wanted to, which I did not. I felt that I must rely on insight in this case and on a certain power I had always possessed of reading faces. That the case called for just this species of intuition I was positive. Mrs. Burton's ruby was within a hundred yards of us at this very moment, probably within a hundred feet; but to lay hands on it and without scandal—well, that was a problem calculated to rouse the interest of even an old police-officer like myself.

A strain of music, desultory, however, and spiritless, like everything else about the place that night, greeted us as Mrs. Ashley opened the door leading directly into the large front hall.

Immediately a scene meant to be festive, but which was, in fact, desolate, burst upon us. The lights, the flowers and the brilliant appearance of such ladies as flitted into sight from the almost empty parlors, were all suggestive of the cheer suitable to a great occasion; but in spite of this, the effect was altogether melancholy, for the hundreds who should have graced this scene, and for whom this illumination had been made and these festoons hung, had been turned away from the gates, and the few who felt they must remain, because their hostess showed no disposition to let them go, wore any but holiday faces, for all their forced smiles and pitiful attempts at nonchalance and gaiety.

I scrutinized these faces carefully. I detected nothing in them but annoyance at a situation which certainly was anything but pleasant.

Turning to Mrs. Ashley, I requested her to be kind enough to point out her son, adding that I should be glad to have a moment's conversation with him, also with Mr. Deane.

"Mr. Deane is in one of those small rooms over there. He is quite upset. Not even Mrs. Burton can comfort him. My son—Oh, there is Harrison!"

A tall, fine-looking young man was crossing the hall. Mrs. Ashley called him to her, and in another moment we were standing together in one of the empty parlors.

I gave him my name and told him my business. Then I said:

"Your mother has allotted me an hour in which to find the valuable jewel which has just been lost on these premises." Here I smiled. "She evidently has great confidence in my ability. I must see that I do not disappoint her."

All this time I was examining his face. It was a handsome one, as I have said, but it had also a very candid expression; the eyes looked straight into mine, and, while showing anxiety, betrayed no deeper emotion than the occasion naturally called for.

"Have you any suggestions to offer? I understand that you were on the ground almost as soon as Mr. Deane discovered his loss."

His eyes changed a trifle but did not swerve. Of course he had been informed by his mother of the suspicious action of the young lady who had been a member of that gentleman's party, and shrank, as any one in his position would, from the responsibilities entailed by this knowledge.

"No," said he. "We have done all we can. The next move must come from you."

"There is one that will settle the matter in a moment," I assured him, still with my eyes fixed scrutinizingly on his face,—"a universal search, not of places, but of persons. But it is a harsh measure."

"A most disagreeable one," he emphasized, flushing. "Such an indignity offered to guests would never be forgotten or forgiven."

"True, but if they offered to submit to this themselves?"

"They? How?"

"If *you*, the son of the house,—their host we may say,—should call them together and, for your own satisfaction, empty out your pockets in the sight of every one, don't you think that all the men, and possibly all the women too—" (here I let my voice fall suggestively) "would be glad to follow suit? It could be done in apparent joke."

He shook his head with a straight-forward air, which raised him high in my estimation.

"That would call for little but effrontery on my part," said he; "but think what it would demand from these boys who came here for the sole purpose of enjoying themselves. I will not so much as mention the ladies."

"Yet one of the latter—"

"I know," he quietly acknowledged, growing restless for the first time.

I withdrew my eyes from his face. I had learned what I wished. Personally he did not shrink from search, therefore the jewel was not in his pockets. This left but two persons for suspicion to halt between. But I disclosed nothing of my thoughts; I merely asked pardon for a suggestion that, while pardonable in a man accustomed to handle crime with ungloved hands, could not fail to prove offensive to a gentleman like himself.

"We must move by means less open," I concluded. "It adds to our difficulties, but that can not be helped. I should now like a glimpse of Mr. Deane."

"Do you not wish to speak to him?"

"I should prefer a sight of his face first."

He led me across the hall and pointed through an open door. In the center of a small room containing a table and some chairs, I perceived a young man sitting, with fallen head and dejected air, staring at vacancy. By his side, with hand laid on his, knelt a young girl, striving in this gentle but speechless way to comfort him. It made a pathetic picture. I drew Ashley away.

"I am disposed to believe in that young man," said I. "If he still has the jewel, he would not try to carry off the situation in just this way. He really looks broken-hearted."

"Oh, he is dreadfully cut up. If you could have seen how frantically he searched for the stone, and the depression into which he fell when he realized that it was not to be found, you would not doubt him for an instant. What made you think he might still have the ruby?"

"Oh, we police officers think of everything. Then the fact that he insists that something or some one touched his breast on the driveway strikes me as a trifle suspicious. Your mother says that no second person could have been there, or the snow would have given evidence of it."

"Yes; I looked expressly. Of course, the drive itself was full of hoof-marks and wheel-tracks, for several carriages had already passed over it. Then there were all of Deane's footsteps, but no other man's, as far as I could see."

"Yet he insists that he was touched or struck."

"Yes."

"With no one there to touch or strike him."

Mr. Ashley was silent.

"Let us step out and take a view of the place," I suggested. "I should prefer doing this to questioning the young man in his present state of mind." Then, as we turned to put on our coats, I asked with suitable precaution: "Do you suppose that he has the same secret suspicions as ourselves, and that it is to hide these he insists upon the jewel's having been taken away from him at a point the ladies are known not to have approached?"

Young Ashley bent somewhat startled eyes on mine.

"Nothing has been said to him of what Miss Peters saw Miss Glover do. I could not bring myself to mention it. I have not even allowed myself to believe—"

Here a fierce gust, blowing in from the door he had just opened, cut short his words, and neither of us spoke again till we stood on the exact spot in the driveway where the episode we were endeavoring to understand had taken place.

"Oh," I cried as soon as I could look about me; "the mystery is explained. Look at that bush, or perhaps you call it a shrub. If the wind were blowing as freshly as it is now, and very probably it was, one of those slender branches might easily be switched against his breast, especially if he stood, as you say he did, close against this border."

"Well, I'm a fool. Only the other day I told the gardener that these branches would need trimming in the spring, and yet I never so much as thought of them when Mr. Deane spoke of something striking his breast."

As we turned back I made this remark:

"With this explanation of the one doubtful point in his otherwise plausible account, we can credit his story as being in the main true, which," I calmly added, "places him above suspicion and narrows our inquiry down to *one*."

We had moved quickly and were now at the threshold of the door by which we had come out.

"Mr. Ashley," I continued, "I shall have to ask you to add to your former favors that of showing me the young lady in whom, from this moment on, we are especially interested. If you can manage to let me see her first without her seeing me, I shall be infinitely obliged to you."

"I do not know where she is. I shall have to search for her."

"I will wait by the hall door."

In a few minutes he returned to me. "Come," said he, and led me into what I judged to be the library.

With a gesture toward one of the windows, he backed quickly out, leaving me to face the situation alone. I was rather glad of this. Glancing in the direction he had indicated, and perceiving the figure of a young lady standing with her back to me on the farther side of a flowing lace curtain, I took a few steps toward her, hoping that the movement would cause her to turn. But it entirely failed to produce this effect, nor did she give any sign that she noted the intrusion. This prevented me from catching the glimpse of her face which I so desired, and obliged me to confine myself to a study of her dress and attitude.

The former was very elegant, more elegant than the appearance of her two friends had led me to expect. Though I am far from being an authority on feminine toilets, I yet had experience enough to know that those sweeping folds of spotless satin, with their festoons of lace and loops of shiny trimming, which it would be folly for me to attempt to describe, represented not only the best efforts of the dressmaker's art, but very considerable means on the part of the woman wearing such a gown. This was a discovery which altered the complexion of my thoughts for a moment; for I had presupposed her a girl of humble means, willing to sacrifice certain scruples to obtain a little extra money. This imposing figure might be that of a millionaire's daughter; how then could I associate her, even in my own mind, with theft? I decided that I must see her face before giving answer to these doubts.

She did not seem inclined to turn. She had raised the shade from before the wintry panes and was engaged in looking out. Her attitude was not that of one simply enjoying a moment's respite from the dance. It was rather that of an absorbed mind brooding upon what gave little or no pleasure; and as I further gazed and noted the droop of her lovely shoulders and the languor visible in her whole bearing, I began to regard a glimpse of her features as imperative. Moving forward, I came upon her suddenly.

"Excuse me, Miss Smith," I boldly exclaimed; then paused, for she had turned instinctively and I had seen that for which I had risked this daring move. "Your pardon," I hastily apologized. "I mistook you for another young lady," and drew back with a low bow to let her pass, for I saw that she thought only of escaping both me and the room.

And I did not wonder at this, for her eyes were streaming with tears, and her face, which was doubtless a pretty one under ordinary conditions, looked so distorted with distracting emotions that she was no fit subject for any man's eye, let alone that of a hard-hearted officer of the law on the lookout for the guilty hand which had just appropriated a jewel worth anywhere from eight to ten thousand dollars.

Yet I was glad to see her weep, for only first offenders weep, and first offenders are amenable to influence, especially if they have been led into wrong by impulse and are weak rather than wicked.

Anxious to make no blunder, I resolved, before proceeding further, to learn what I could of the character and antecedents of the suspected one, and this from the only source which offered—Mr. Deane's affianced.

This young lady was a delicate girl, with a face like a flower. Recognizing her sensitive nature, I approached her with the utmost gentleness. Not seeking to disguise either the nature of my business or my reasons for being in the house, since all this gave me authority, I modulated my tone to suit her gentle spirit, and, above all, I showed the utmost sympathy for her lover, whose rights in the reward had been taken from him as certainly as the jewel had been taken from Mrs. Burton. In this way I gained her confidence, and she was quite ready to listen when I observed:

"There is a young lady here who seems to be in a state of even greater trouble than Mr. Deane. Why is this? You brought her here. Is her sympathy with Mr. Deane so great as to cause her to weep over his loss?"

"Frances? Oh, no. She likes Mr. Deane and she likes me, but not well enough to cry over our misfortunes. I think she has some trouble of her own."

"One that you can tell me?"

Her surprise was manifest.

"Why do you ask that? What interest have you (called in, as I understand, to recover a stolen jewel) in Frances Glover's personal difficulties?"

I saw that I must make my position perfectly plain.

"Only this. She was seen to pick up something from the driveway, where no one else had succeeded in finding anything."

"She? When? Who saw her?"

"I can not answer all these questions at once," I smiled. "She was seen to do this—no matter by whom,—during your passage from the carriage to the stoop. As you preceded her, you naturally did not observe this action, which was fortunate, perhaps, as you would scarcely have known what to do or say about it."

"Yes I should," she retorted, with a most unexpected display of spirit. "I should have asked her what she had found and I should have insisted upon an answer. I love my friends, but I love the man I am to marry, better." Here her voice fell and a most becoming blush suffused her cheek.

"Quite right," I assented. "Now will you answer my former question? What troubles Miss Glover? Can you tell me?"

"That I can not. I only know that she has been very silent ever since she left the house. I thought her beautiful new dress would please her, but it does not seem to. She has been unhappy and preoccupied all the evening. She only roused a bit when Mr. Deane showed us the ruby and said—Oh, I forgot!"

"What's that? What have you forgot?"

"What you said just now. I wouldn't add a word—"

"Pardon me!" I smilingly interrupted, looking as fatherly as I could, "but you *have* added this word and now you must tell me what it means. You were going to say she showed interest in the extraordinary jewel which Mr. Deane took from his pocket and—"

"In what he let fall about the expected reward. That is, she looked eagerly at the ruby and sighed when he acknowledged that he expected it to bring him five hundred dollars before midnight. But any girl of no more means than she might do that. It would not be fair to lay too much stress on a sigh."

"Is not Miss Glover wealthy? She wears a very expensive dress, I observe."

"I know it and I have wondered a little at it, for her father is not called very well off. But perhaps she bought it with her own money; I know she has some; she is an artist in burnt wood."

I let the subject of Miss Glover's dress drop. I had heard enough to satisfy me that my first theory was correct. This young woman, beautifully dressed, and with a face from which the rounded lines of early girlhood had not yet departed, held in her possession, probably at this very moment, Mrs. Burton's magnificent jewel. But where? On her person or hidden in some of her belongings? I remembered the cloak in the closet and thought it wise to assure myself that the jewel was not secreted in this garment, before I proceeded to extreme measures. Mrs. Ashley, upon being consulted, agreed with me as to the desirability of this, and presently I had this poor girl's cloak in my hands.

Did I find the ruby? No; but I found something else tucked away in an inner pocket which struck me as bearing quite pointedly upon this case. It was the bill—crumpled, soiled and tear-stained—of the dress whose elegance had so surprised her friends and made me, for a short time, regard her as the daughter of wealthy parents. An enormous bill, which must have struck dismay to the soul of this self-supporting girl, who probably had no idea of how a French dressmaker can foot up items. Four hundred and fifty dollars! and for one gown! I declare I felt indignant myself and could quite understand why she heaved that little sigh when Mr. Deane spoke of the five hundred dollars he expected from Mrs. Burton, and later, how she came to succumb to the temptation of making the effort to secure this sum for herself when, in following the latter's footsteps up the driveway, she stumbled upon this same jewel fallen, as it were, from his pocket into her very hands. The impulse of the moment was so strong and the consequences so little anticipated!

It is not at all probable that she foresaw he would shout aloud his loss and draw the whole household out on the porch. Of course when he did this, the feasibility of her project was gone, and I only wished that I had been present and able to note her countenance, as, crowded in with others on that windy porch, she watched the progress of the search, which every moment made it not only less impossible for her to attempt the restoration upon which the reward depended, but must have caused her to feel, if she had been as well brought up as all indications showed, that it was a dishonest act of which she had been guilty and that, willing or not, she must look upon herself as a thief so long as she held the jewel back from Mr. Deane or its rightful owner. But how face the publicity of restoring it now, after this elaborate and painful search, in which even the son of her hostess had taken part?

That would be to proclaim her guilt and thus effectually ruin her in the eyes of everybody concerned. No, she would keep the compromising article a little longer, in the hope of finding some opportunity of returning it without risk to her good name. And so she allowed the search to proceed.

I have entered thus elaborately into the supposed condition of this girl's mind on this critical evening, that you may understand why I felt a certain sympathy for her, which forbade harsh measures. I was sure, from the glimpse I had caught of her face, that she longed to be relieved from the tension she was under, and that she would gladly rid herself of this valuable jewel if she only knew how. This opportunity I proposed to give her; and this is why, on returning the bill to its place, I assumed such an air of relief on rejoining Mrs. Ashley.

She saw, and drew me aside.

"You have not found it!" she said.

"No," I returned, "but I am positive where it is."

"And where is that?"

"Over Miss Glover's uneasy heart."

Mrs. Ashley turned pale.

"Wait," said I; "I have a scheme for getting it hence without making her shame public. Listen!" and I whispered a few words in her ear.

She surveyed me in amazement for a moment, then nodded, and her face lighted up.

"You are certainly earning your reward," she declared; and summoning her son, who was never far away from her side, she whispered her wishes. He started, bowed and hurried from the room.

By this time my business in the house was well-known to all, and I could not appear in hall or parlor without a great silence falling upon every one present, followed by a breaking up of the only too small circle of unhappy guests into agitated groups. But I appeared to see nothing of all this till the proper moment, when, turning suddenly upon them all, I cried out cheerfully, but with a certain deference I thought would please them:

"Ladies and gentlemen: I have an interesting fact to announce. The snow which was taken up from the driveway has been put to melt in the great feed caldron over the stable fire. We expect to find the ruby at the bottom, and Mrs. Ashley invites you to be present at its recovery. It has now stopped snowing and she thought you might enjoy the excitement of watching the water ladled out."

A dozen girls bounded forward.

"Oh, yes, what fun! where are our cloaks—our rubbers?"

Two only stood hesitating. One of these was Mr. Deane's lady love and the other her friend, Miss Glover. The former, perhaps, secretly wondered. The latter—but I dared not look long enough or closely enough in her direction to judge just what her emotions were. Presently these, too, stepped forward into the excited circle of young people, and were met by the two maids who were bringing in their wraps. Amid the bustle which now ensued, I caught sight of Mr. Deane's face peering from an open doorway. It was all alive with hope. I also perceived a lady looking down from the second story, who, I felt sure, was Mrs. Burton herself. Evidently my confident tone had produced more effect than the words themselves. Every one looked upon the jewel as already recovered and regarded my invitation to the stable as a ruse by which I hoped to restore universal good feeling by giving them all a share in my triumph.

All but one! Nothing could make Miss Glover look otherwise than anxious, restless and unsettled, and though she followed in the wake of the rest, it was with hidden face and lagging step, as if she recognized the whole thing as a farce and doubted her own power to go through it calmly.

"Ah, ha! my lady," thought I, "only be patient and you will see what I shall do for you." And indeed I thought her eye brightened as we all drew up around the huge caldron standing full of water over the stable stove. As pains had already been taken to put out the fire in this stove, the ladies were not afraid of injuring their dresses and consequently crowded as close as their numbers would permit. Miss Glover especially stood within reach of the brim, and as soon as I noted this, I gave the signal which had been agreed upon between Mr. Ashley and myself. Instantly the electric lights went out, leaving the place in total darkness.

A scream from the girls, a burst of hilarious laughter from their escorts, mingled with loud apologies from their seemingly mischievous host, filled up the interval of darkness which I had insisted should not be too soon curtailed; then the lights glowed as suddenly as they had gone out, and while the glare was fresh on every face, I stole a glance at Miss Glover to see if she had made good use of the opportunity just accorded for ridding herself of the jewel by dropping it into the caldron. If she had, both her troubles and mine were at an end; if she had not, then I need feel no further scruple in approaching her with the direct question I had hitherto found it so difficult to put.

She stood with both hands grasping her cloak which she had drawn tightly about the rich folds of her new and expensive dress; but her eyes were fixed straight before her with a soft light in their depths which made her positively beautiful.

The jewel is in the pot, I inwardly decided, and ordered the two waiting stablemen to step forward with their ladles. Quickly those ladles went in, but before they could be lifted out dripping, half the ladies had scurried back, afraid of injury to their pretty dresses. But they soon sidled forward again, and watched with beaming eyes the slow but sure emptying of the great caldron at whose bottom they anticipated finding the lost jewel.

As the ladles were plunged deeper and deeper, the heads drew closer and so great was the interest shown, that the busiest lips forgot to chatter, and eyes, whose only business up till now had been to follow with shy curiosity every motion made by their handsome young host, now settled on the murky depths of the great pot whose bottom was almost in sight.

As I heard the ladles strike this bottom, I instinctively withdrew a step in anticipation of the loud hurrah which would naturally hail the first sight of the lost ruby. Conceive, then, my chagrin, my bitter and mortified disappointment, when, after one look at the broad surface of the now exposed bottom the one shout which rose was:

"Nothing!"

I was so thoroughly put out that I did not wait to hear the loud complaints which burst from every lip. Drawing Mr. Ashley aside (who, by the way, seemed as much affected as myself by the turn affairs had taken) I remarked to him that there was only one course left open to us.

"And what is that?"

"To ask Miss Glover to show me what she picked up from your driveway."

"And if she refuses?"

"To take her quietly with me to the station, where we have women who can make sure that the ruby is not on her person."

Mr. Ashley made an involuntary gesture of strong repugnance.

"Let us pray that it will not come to that," he objected hoarsely. "Such a fine figure of a girl! Did you notice how bright and happy she looked when the lights sprang up? I declare she struck me as lovely."

"So she did me, and caused me to draw some erroneous conclusions. I shall have to ask you to procure me an interview with her as soon as we return to the house."

"She shall meet you in the library."

But when, a few minutes later, she joined me in the room just designated and I had full opportunity for reading her countenance, I own that my task became suddenly hateful to me. She was not far from my own daughter's age and, had it not been for her furtive look of care, appeared almost as blooming and bright. Would it ever come to pass that a harsh man of the law would feel it his duty to speak to my Flora as I must now speak to the young girl before me? The thought made me inwardly recoil and it was in as gentle a manner as possible that I made my bow and began with the following remark:

"I hope you will pardon me, Miss Glover—I am told that is your name. I hate to disturb your pleasure—" (this with the tears of alarm and grief rising in her eyes) "but you can tell me something which will greatly simplify my task and possibly put matters in such shape that you and your friends can be released to your homes."

"I?"

She stood before me with amazed eyes, the color rising in her cheeks. I had to force my next words, which, out of consideration for her, I made as direct as possible.

"Yes, miss. What was the article you were seen to pick up from the driveway soon after leaving your carriage?"

She started, then stumbled backward, tripping in her long train.

"I pick up?" she murmured. Then with a blush, whether of anger or pride I could not tell, she coldly answered: "Oh, that was something of my own,—something I had just dropped. I had rather not tell you what it was."

I scrutinized her closely. She met my eyes squarely, yet not with just the clear light I should, remembering Flora, have been glad to see there.

"I think it would be better for you to be entirely frank," said I. "It was the only article known to have been picked up from the driveway after Mr. Deane's loss of the ruby; and though we do not presume to say that it was the ruby, yet the matter would look clearer to us all if you would frankly state what this object was."

Her whole body seemed to collapse and she looked as if about to sink.

"Oh, where is Minnie? Where is Mr. Deane?" she moaned, turning and staring at the door, as if she hoped they would fly to her aid. Then, in a burst of indignation which I was fain to believe real, she turned on me with the cry: "It was a bit of paper which I had thrust into the bosom of my gown. It fell out—"

"Your dressmaker's bill?" I intimated.

She stared, laughed hysterically for a moment, then sank upon a near-by sofa, sobbing spasmodically.

"Yes," she cried, after a moment; "my dressmaker's bill. You seem to know all my affairs." Then suddenly, and with a startling impetuosity, which drew her to her feet: "Are you going to tell everybody that? Are you going to state publicly that Miss Glover brought an unpaid bill to the party and that because Mr. Deane was unfortunate enough or careless enough to drop and lose the jewel he was bringing to Mrs. Burton, she is to be looked upon as a thief, because she stooped to pick up this bill which had slipped inadvertently from its hiding-place? I shall die if you do," she cried. "I shall die if it is already known," she pursued, with increasing emotion. "Is it? Is it?"

Her passion was so great, so much greater than any likely to rise in a breast wholly innocent, that I began to feel very sober.

"No one but Mrs. Ashley and possibly her son know about the bill," said I, "and no one shall, if you will go with that lady to her room, and make plain to her, in the only way you can, that the extremely valuable article which has been lost to-night is not in your possession."

She threw up her arms with a scream. "Oh, what a horror! I can not! I can not! Oh, I shall die of shame! My father! My mother!" And she burst from the room like one distraught.

But in another moment she came cringing back. "I can not face them," she said. "They all believe it; they will always believe it unless I submit—Oh, why did I ever come to this dreadful place? Why did I order this hateful dress which I can never pay for and which, in spite of the misery it has caused me, has failed to bring me the—" She did not continue. She had caught my eye and seen there, perhaps, some evidence of the pity I could not but experience for her. With a sudden change of tone she advanced upon me with the appeal: "Save me from this humiliation. I have not seen the ruby. I am as ignorant of its whereabouts as—as Mr. Ashley himself. Won't you believe me? Won't they be satisfied if I swear—"

I was really sorry for her. I began to think too that some dreadful mistake had been made. Her manner seemed too ingenuous for guilt. Yet where could that ruby be, if not with this young girl? Certainly, all other possibilities had been exhausted, and her story of the bill, even if accepted, would never quite exonerate her from secret suspicion while that elusive jewel remained unfound.

"You give me no hope," she moaned. "I must go out before them all and ask to have it proved that I am no thief. Oh, if God would have pity—"

"Or some one would find—Halloo! What's that?"

A shout had risen from the hall beyond.

She gasped and we both plunged forward. Mr. Ashley, still in his overcoat, stood at the other end of the hall, and facing him were ranged the whole line of young people whom I had left scattered about in the various parlors. I thought he looked peculiar; certainly his appearance differed from that of a quarter of an hour before, and when he glanced our way and saw who was standing with me in the library doorway, his voice took on a tone which made me doubt whether he was about to announce good news or bad.

But his first word settled that question.

"Rejoice with me!" he cried. "*The ruby has been found!* Do you want to see the culprit?—for there is a culprit. We have him at the door; shall we bring him in?"

"Yes, yes," cried several voices, among them that of Mr. Deane, who now strode forward with beaming eyes and instinctively lifted hand. But some of the ladies looked frightened, and Mr. Ashley, noting this, glanced for encouragement toward us.

He seemed to find it in Miss Glover's eyes. She had quivered and nearly fallen at that word *found*, but had drawn herself up by this time and was awaiting his further action in a fever of relief and hope which perhaps no one but myself could fully appreciate.

"A vile thief! A most unconscionable rascal!" vociferated Mr. Ashley. "You must see him, mother; you must see him, ladies, else you will not realize our good fortune. Open the door there and bring in the robber!"

At this command, uttered in ringing tones, the huge leaves of the great front door swung slowly forward, revealing the sturdy forms of the two stablemen holding down by main force the towering figure of—*a horse!*

The scream of astonishment which went up from all sides, united to Mr. Ashley's shout of hilarity, caused the animal, unused, no doubt, to drawing-rooms, to rear to the length of his bridle. At which Mr. Ashley laughed again and gaily cried:

"Confound the fellow! Look at him, mother; look at him, ladies! Do you not see guilt written on his brow? It is he who has made us all this trouble. First, he must needs take umbrage at the two lights with which we presumed to illuminate our porch; then, envying Mrs. Burton her ruby and Mr. Deane his reward, seek to rob them both by grinding his hoofs all over the snow of the driveway till he came upon the jewel which Mr. Deane had dropped from his pocket, and taking it up in a ball of snow, secrete it in his left hind shoe,—where it might be yet, if Mr. Spencer—" here he bowed to a strange gentleman who at that moment entered—"had not come himself for his daughters, and, going first to the stable, found his horse so restless and seemingly lame—(there, boys, you may take the wretch away now and harness him, but first hold up that guilty left hind hoof for the ladies to see)— that he stooped to examine him, and so came upon *this*."

Here the young gentleman brought forward his hand. In it was a nondescript little wad, well soaked and shapeless; but, once he had untied the kid, such a ray of rosy light burst from his outstretched palm that I doubt if a single woman there noted the clatter of the retiring beast or the heavy clang made by the two front doors as they shut upon the *robber*. Eyes and tongues were too busy, and Mr. Ashley, realizing, probably, that the interest of all present would remain, for a few minutes at least, with this marvelous jewel so astonishingly recovered, laid it, with many expressions of thankfulness, in Mrs. Burton's now eagerly outstretched palm, and advancing toward us, paused in front of Miss Glover and eagerly held out his hand.

"Congratulate me," he prayed. "All our troubles are over—Oh, what now!"

The poor young thing, in trying to smile, had turned as white as a sheet. Before either of us could interpose an arm, she had slipped to the floor in a dead faint. With a murmur of pity and possibly of inward contrition, he stooped over her and together we carried her into the library, where I left her in his care, confident, from certain indications, that my presence would not be greatly missed by either of them.

Whatever hope I may have had of reaping the reward offered by Mrs. Ashley was now lost, but, in the satisfaction I experienced at finding this young girl as innocent as my Flora, I did not greatly care.

Well, it all ended even more happily than may here appear. The horse not putting in his claim to the reward, and Mr. Spencer repudiating all right to it, it was paid in full to Mr. Deane, who went home in as buoyant a state of mind as was possible to him after the great anxieties of the preceding two hours. Miss Glover was sent back by the Ashleys in their own carriage and I was told that Mr. Ashley declined to close the carriage door upon her till she had promised to come again the following night.

Anxious to make such amends as I personally could for my share in the mortification to which she had been subjected, I visited her in the morning, with the intention of offering a suggestion or two in regard to that little bill. But she met my first advance with a radiant smile and the glad exclamation:

"Oh, I have settled all that! I have just come from Madame Duprè's. I told her that I had never imagined the dress could possibly cost more than a hundred dollars, and I offered her that sum if she would take the garment back. And she did, she did, and I shall never have to wear that dreadful satin again."

I made a note of this dressmaker's name. She and I may have a bone to pick some day. But I said nothing to Miss Glover. I merely exclaimed:

"And to-night?"

"Oh, I have an old spotted muslin which, with a few natural flowers, will make me look festive enough. One does not need fine clothes when one is—happy."

The dreamy far-off smile with which she finished the sentence was more eloquent than words, and I was not surprised when some time later I read of her engagement to Mr. Ashley.

But it was not till she could sign herself with his name that she told me just what underlay the misery of that night. She had met Harrison Ashley more than once before, and, though she did not say so, had evidently conceived an admiration for him which made her especially desirous of attracting and pleasing him. Not understanding the world very well, certainly having very little knowledge of the tastes and feelings of wealthy people, she conceived that the more brilliantly she was attired the more likely she would be to please this rich young man. So in a moment of weakness she decided to devote all her small savings (a hundred dollars, as we know) to buying a gown such as she felt she could appear in at his house without shame.

It came home, as dresses from French dressmakers are very apt to do, just in time for her to put it on for the party. The bill came with it and when she saw the amount—it was all itemized and she could find no fault with anything but the summing up—she was so overwhelmed that she nearly fainted. But she could not give up her ball; so she dressed herself, and, being urged all the time to hurry, hardly stopped to give one look at the new and splendid gown which had cost so much. The bill—the incredible, the enormous bill—was all she could think of, and the figures, which represented nearly her whole year's earnings, danced constantly before her eyes. How to pay it—but she could not pay it, nor could she ask her father to do so. She was ruined; but the ball, and Mr. Ashley—these still awaited her; so presently she worked herself up to some anticipation of enjoyment, and, having thrown on her cloak, was turning down her light preparatory to departure, when her eye fell on the bill lying open on her dresser.

It would never do to leave it there—never do to leave it anywhere in her room. There were prying eyes in the house, and she was as ashamed of that bill as she might have been of a contemplated theft. So she tucked it in her corsage and went down to join her friends in the carriage.

The rest we know, all but one small detail which turned to gall whatever enjoyment she was able to get out of the early evening. There was a young girl present, dressed in a simple muslin gown. While looking at it and inwardly contrasting it with her own splendor, Mr. Ashley passed by with another gentleman and she heard him say:

"How much better young girls look in simple white than in the elaborate silks only suitable for their mothers!"

Thoughtless words, possibly forgotten as soon as uttered, but they sharply pierced this already sufficiently stricken and uneasy breast and were the cause of the tears which had aroused my suspicion when I came upon her in the library, standing with her face to the night.

But who can say whether, if the evening had been devoid of these occurrences and no emotions of contrition and pity had been awakened in her behalf in the breast of her chivalrous host, she would ever have become Mrs. Ashley?

Lector House believes that a society develops through a two-fold approach of continuous learning and adaptation, which is derived from the study of classic literary works spread across the historic timeline of literature records. Therefore, we aim at reviving, repairing and redeveloping all those inaccessible or damaged but historically as well as culturally important literature across subjects so that the future generations may have an opportunity to study and learn from past works to embark upon a journey of creating a better future.

This book is a result of an effort made by Lector House towards making a contribution to the preservation and repair of original ancient works which might hold historical significance to the approach of continuous learning across subjects.

HAPPY READING & LEARNING!

LECTOR HOUSE LLP
E-MAIL: lectorpublishing@gmail.com